Contents

Foreword

Some seven or eight years ago a new author of 'science fiction' emerged; Anthony Fucilla. (I include the inverted commas here because his writing is so much more than just science fiction.) His first book, *Quantum Chronicles in the Eleventh Dimension*, consisted of what appeared at first sight to be a series of science fiction short stories, but further, deeper examination revealed much more in those stories. The underlying science used was either well-known or prophetically speculative. They showed at once an author who had thought long and deeply before putting pen to paper. The end result was to leave readers eagerly anticipating a future volume. When the anticipated second volume did emerge, the readers were not disappointed. In fact, many felt the second volume better than the first. However, once again the reader was left to wonder as to the true purpose of the writer because the tales in both volumes went so much further academically than many conventional science fiction texts; they delved unashamedly into the realms of both philosophy and, maybe a little surprisingly to some, theology. In both of the earlier volumes, the author will undoubtedly have alienated some by his extremely brave approach to even bringing issues of theology so overtly into his writing. However, I believe the author was not only eager to have his work read but, possibly more importantly, wished his readers to ponder and reflect later on the deeper issues about which they had been reading. So what of this third volume?

It is not, I think, the task of a Forward to unlock the delights of the book to follow, but rather to try to whet the appetites of potential readers. Hence, I will make no attempt to comment on any of the individual stories. Suffice it say, therefore, that this latest collection does not disappoint. The overall theme is the same; an attempt to raise deep, important issues of philosophy and theology via the medium of science fiction. Does the writer succeed? Yes; I can confidently say that, as in his earlier books, he does, but this time he is probably even braver in highlighting some new sources of misery for mankind. Yet again, he will annoy some by the line he takes but I would urge people of all views and beliefs to read these stories – and the previous two volumes if they haven't done so already – as, whatever your basic belief, you will benefit from reading this body of work if you approach it with an open mind and are prepared to reflect and contemplate on what you have read at leisure later. I assure all that such an experience will not be unrewarding. However, for any who simply wish to read some science fiction stories for their own sake, again you will enjoy a pleasurable read but I would urge potential readers to take that extra step and ponder on what they've read at a later time; the end result will make the little intellectual effort so worthwhile. I hope all enjoy and benefit from reading this delightful collection of short stories.

Professor Jeremy Dunning-Davies.

This book is dedicated to my beautiful baby daughter Kristina Elaine and my grandmother Iolina...

Mechanical Brain Wave

FELIX Hieronymus placed the electrodes of the sleep-inducer on his forehead. It was set for an hour's sleep. He lay back on his flexi-chair and could feel the gentle electronic pulses. He closed his eyes, and slowly darkness began to invade his consciousness. In dream states time alters its properties, he thought sluggishly. It's psychological... but that's all there is. As the electronic pulses continued to surge softly through his brain, consciousness faded. An hour later the alarm sounded and he awoke. Slowly, he made his way into the living room of his apartment. Instantly the body heat sensor vision screen lit up. A space documentary was playing. He could see a ship preparing for take-off. As the ship fired into the blue of the atmosphere, heading for the eternal darkness of space, he could see the dull red glow from the radiation fins around the vessel's equator, as the heat loss from the mass-converters was promptly dissipated into space. As the ship achieved escape velocity, 25,000 miles an hour, it severed the umbilical cord gravity and was free. Next he saw a close up image of the sun; a fiery ball of eternal fire twisting and turning in the magnetic fields of its own creation.

The images roused his interest; he now wanted to test his new computer - a scientific and mathematical masterpiece. It was built to answer the most mysterious and complex questions. He wanted to test it to see how efficient Socrates really was. Instantly he made his way into his small dimly lit study and sat. To his left was an open window from where he could clearly see the Moon, pale and bleached against the blackness beyond; It hung over the face of the Pacific like a jewel. A sudden gust of cross wind slapped the window. He refocused, and adjusted himself, and was now ready. He checked his watch: the dials read 22:45. As power entered the small grey computer, mechanical consciousness, the screen lit up and a 3-dimensional face formed with a speed perceptible to the eye:

"Good evening Felix Hieronymus. What can I help you with?"

"How did you know my name?" His field of vision contracted until it embraced only the face on the screen.

"You already seek to trap me into an inconsistency."

"What do you mean?"

"I'm not called Socrates for no reason. When you speak on the phone, even though I'm switched off, I still register sound waves and store all information. In essence I'm always conscious."

Felix smiled.

"Okay, let's start again. Good evening Socrates."

"Good evening Felix."

"Tell me, could a human being ever be miniaturized? Say in order to perform a particular task?"

"Biological miniaturization is scientifically impossible. There would not be enough atoms in their tiny brains to make the brain complex enough to be a human brain. This whole notion belongs to the realms of fantasy."

"A great theologian once told me that consciousness can only be explained in theological terms: that is, that spark, consciousness, is connected to the fact that God breathed life into man, and as a result, man became a living being: quote Acts 17:28... *For in him we live and move and have our being.* In your opinion, what is consciousness? How would you define it?"

"Consciousness is the continual creation of models, feedback loops, which describe a model of our place in space-time."

"How does animal consciousness differ from human?"

"Animals have no perception of time, the future."

"How does human consciousness differ from a robot – like you for example?"

"A robot is more intelligent...."

Felix smiled.

"In regards to epistemology, tell me, what is knowledge and how can it be acquired?"

"Knowledge means to acquire information, and process that information using the mind. Reason and logic automatically help us to understand the data acquired. In basic terms, existence means to attain knowledge. Every person attains a certain amount of knowledge via their senses, as he goes through the journey of life; some more than others. However, there is another form, which I describe as inbuilt, within the DNA. That is, some people are genetically predisposed to knowledge and geniality. It's a knowledge that is not acquired but is inbuilt at a cellular level."

"Ok, what are premonitions?"

"Most premonitions can be explained by coincidence. Even the most improbable events will occur if you wait long enough. The laws of chance do not merely permit coincidence; they compel them. However, premonitions may be subconscious foresight: warnings of danger that the senses have detected. In summary, premonitions are warnings from the human mind."

"Ok, now tell me about the birth of the universe...."

"The big bang created time and space. It occurred some 13.8 billion years ago. Then the universe was infinitely hot and dense before cooling and expanding. One trillionth of a second after the explosion – the big bang - the weak and electromagnetic forces separated, leaving us with the four major cosmic forces that we know today – strong, weak, electromagnetic and gravity. One hundred seconds after the big bang, the temperature dropped to the point where protons and neutrons (subatomic particles) could stick together without being torn apart. Here the universe was made mostly of photons – which are particles of light. Hydrogen then formed. After some 380,000 years, the opaque soup began to clear and, since the temperature of the universe had dropped to 3,000 Kelvin (2,727 - Celsius), photons were travelling through the universe, free from matter. The lack of high temperatures and intense radiation meant that atoms could form from electrons and protons without being ripped apart, and the universe became transparent. Gravitational attraction between atoms brought them into faint clouds of gas. One billion years after the initial explosion (big bang), the first stars and galaxies were formed. Due to the expanding universe, galaxies are racing further and further apart. Most galaxies are moving away from us."

"When was the Sun formed?"

Approximately 9 billion years after the Big Bang, our sun formed from a large cloud of gas and dust. As the Sun was forming, a disc of leftover gas and dust was created around it. Over a period of hundreds of millions of years, the planets grew, forming the Solar System."

"Ok, how will the universe end in your opinion?"

"There are three possible ways: One is known as the Big Crunch – Closed Universe. The density of the universe is more than 5 atoms of hydrogen per cubic metre. There's no repulsive effect of dark energy and gravity eventually halts the universe's expansion. With contraction, all the matter in the universe collapses to a point. This as mentioned, is known as the Big Crunch. The other is known as the Big Rip – Open Universe. If space is curved and open, the universe in principle will continue to expand forever. Of course, dark energy will help drive the expansion. As a result of this, there is heat death. The Big Rip or Big Freeze will take place. Finally: The Flat Universe. With no dark energy, a flat universe will expand forever at a decelerating rate. With dark energy the expansion initially slows. This is due to gravity. It then speeds up. The Universe's ultimate fate is the same as the Open Universe theory: The Big Freeze – Big Rip."

"Ok... What's the difference between an asteroid and a dwarf planet?"

"It all comes down to its shape. To be a dwarf planet, a body must have sufficient mass to achieve hydrostatic equilibrium, when it will become spherical."

"Tell me about Terrestrial planets."

"These types of Planets are rocky with metal cores and high densities... Mars and Earth are good examples. They are much smaller than the Gas Giants, and have slower rotation periods. They are also less likely to have moons due to their smaller size."

"How big is Jupiter compared with Earth?"

"Jupiter is 11 times larger than Earth, and has a volume 1,300 times greater. Its average distance from the sun is 483.6 million miles. The number of moon's it has is 63. Surface temperature on Jupiter is -110 Celsius. "

Felix's desire to continue to test the computer's efficiency and intelligence was growing as he sat in silence.

"Tell me about the spiral galaxy Andromeda."

"Andromeda and its 100 million stars, is over two million light years away from Earth. However they are rapidly getting closer. They are moving towards us at a speed of 402,000 kilometres per hour, which equates to 250,000 miles per hour, on a course for collision 4 billion years from now."

"Tell me about hypervelocity stars."

"They travel at speeds of over 3.2 million kilometres per hour. At this velocity, they are fast enough to escape the gravitational pull of their parent planet."

"How much of the universe is thought to be composed of Dark Matter?"

"Roughly 25/26 per cent of the universe is thought to be composed of dark matter, made up of subatomic particles that interact weakly with ordinary matter."

"What is the Tarantula Nebula made from?"

"The wispy arms of the Nebula are made from partially ionised hydrogen gas, excited by a supercluster of massive stars called R136. It is the largest star forming region in nearby space: hidden within it are more than 800,000 new stars."

"Tell me about Dark energy."

"Dark energy, which accounts for roughly 70 per cent of the universe, is the driving force behind why galaxies are moving away from us in an almost eternal expansion. Nobody really knows what dark energy is, or even how strong it is. It acts like anti-gravity pushing the universe apart. As the gravity of dark matter tries to pull the universe together, dark energy tries to push it apart. Approximately 5 billion years ago, the early universe was totally dominated by dark matter. As the universe ages, it starts to expand further out. The domination of dark energy thus increases."

"Tell me, if a black hole is sitting at the centre of its galaxy, does it distort the fabric of the universe around it?"

"Yes. Yes, it leaves a dent in this sheet of space-time from which nothing can escape, not even light. Funnels made by the black hole twisting the space-time fabric suck up particles, which are accelerated by electric currents, before being blown out into space as beams of radiation and charged particles."

"Tell me more about black holes..."

"Well Felix, many black holes started life as stars. Stars spend the whole duration of stellar-life resisting gravitational collapse. For example, their huge mass means that the gas is constantly pulled towards the core. Instead of collapsing down, atoms collide and fuse. As a result explosive atomic energy is released. Radiation pushes outwards against gravity, holding the star open as a glowing ball of gas. As a star ages, more of the atoms are fused, thus creating heavier elements, and eventually the fuel starts to diminish. Without the outward push, the balance is tipped in favour of the immutable force – gravity, and the star begins to collapse. Eventually, a dense neutron star, or black hole, is formed. Black holes slow the flow of time.

They have no size limit. In fact, Supermassive black holes contain the mass of at least 100,000 Suns compressed into a space that is around the size of our solar system. The event horizon of a black hole can measure thousands of kilometres in diameter. What actually takes place with a black hole is open to much debate. However, the curvature of space-time inside a black hole is directed towards a single point, known mathematically as a singularity. Some black holes spin at half the speed of light. Spinning black holes distort space-time, wrapping it into a swirl known as the ergosphere."

"Can particle accelerations create a micro black hole?"

"Particles travelling close to the speed of light could theoretically produce mini black holes. These mini black holes, as well as opening portals into different dimensions, could be produced inside the Hadron Collider."

"Tell me about the two main Cosmic Forces that control our universe...."

"Let's start with Gravity: It influences all objects with mass, and is responsible for everything from the falling mountain rock to the orbit of a planet. In comparison with other fundamental forces, gravity is actually very weak. It only makes its presence felt when matter is present in large amounts. However it does operate over large ranges. Gravity is also known to distort space and time. Planetary orbits like that of Mars around the Sun can be thought of as 'dents' in space-time. An effect known as gravitational lensing is key evidence for the way gravity operates. In short, it involves the deflection of mass-less light from distant stars as it passes close to nearby huge objects. Like the Sun for example. The other force is electromagnetism: It is stronger than the force of gravity, but the range of its effects is less. Electricity is simply the flow of charged particles (atoms), while magnetic forces act on electrically charged particles inside certain objects. Light and all types of radiation such as X-rays and infrared, are electromagnetic waves generated by materials that are heated, for example the surface of a star. Photons which are wave particles are responsible for transmitting electromagnetic forces across space at the speed of light. The Sun, the massive nuclear reactor, has an enormous and very powerful magnetic field. This is created by the movement of huge masses of electrically charged plasma (hot gas) beneath its surface."

"Do wormholes exist...?"

"I know you expect a definitive answer Felix, but the truth is I'm not certain whether traversable wormholes really exist. These gateways or tunnels that provide a shortcut through the fabric of space-time may exist, but I can't be certain. "

"Ok fine, but tell me about the making of a wormhole..."

"Firstly Felix, when a gigantic star eventually succumbs to entropy – that is the star dies, and when it no longer has any nuclear fuel to burn, sometimes a black hole is formed; The core has no choice but to collapse in on itself in the catastrophic explosion of a supernova. The star's outer layers are expelled into space. Regarding the core, it will continue to shrink in size, getting smaller and smaller. As it shrinks into a tiny speck, all of its mass is concentrated in a very small area. This forms a singularity. Although small, it is very heavy and it can bend space-time. A star's core can still be found spinning when it decides to collapse. Disintegrating to a singularity, it rotates faster and faster. In fact, it spins so fast that what's left of the star's material spreads out. Space-time is no longer focused on a single point, but is being wrapped around a space-ring. As the tunnel is formed, it punches its way through the fabric of space-time and, almost in an unusual state of reversal, emerges backwards in time and into the past. This tunnel, which can work its way into another parallel universe, is called a wormhole."

"So in theory you could turn a wormhole into a time machine?"

"Yes, however, in order to hold the wormhole open, or to enlarge its mouth, especially if a spaceship was to pass through, you would require something called exotic matter. Basically, this is something with negative energy to act as anti-gravity. Between the two mouths of the wormhole is a tunnel that acts as the bridge across space and time."

"How would you define a planet?"

"A planet has to have enough mass that its self-gravity causes it to reach hydrostatic equilibrium. Thus - the planet is able to resist comprehensive forces in space to hold together. In other words – it is bound together by gravity. Finally, a planet is a large non-stellar body in orbit around a star, shining only by reflecting the star's light."

"How would you measure our solar system?"

"Via Radar... Astronomers, time how long it takes the radar beam, which is travelling at the speed of light, to travel the distance to an object and back. By multiplying the speed of light by the time taken, then dividing that in two, astronomers can derive the distance to the object. Once the distance has been attained, the mass of the object can be ascertained via monitoring the orbital periods of circling satellites. In order to achieve this, scientists have to measure the angular separation between the satellite and the object. They then have to use trigonometry in order to convert that angular separation into distance. The total mass is finally determined by using Kepler's third law."

"Ok... tell me a little bit about NASA'S Terra Satellite."

"It investigates the impact of natural and man-made climate changes. It travels in a north-to-south, near-polar orbit at an altitude of 705km. It views the entire surface of earth every two days."

Felix was gripped in deep thought....

"Could we ever live on the Moon?"

"Yes, however: you would need to grow food there. This would mean importing chemicals that aren't available on the surface or in the atmosphere. In order to obtain power: solar panels are best, but, on most places on the Moon, the Sun only shines for part of the time, and so storage facilities and other sources of power would be needed. Electricity might also come from a nuclear plant or fuel cells, using elements found on the surface of the Moon."

"Tell me about the moon during a lunar eclipse...."

"Unlike a solar eclipse, which hides the sun, you can still see the Moon in a total lunar eclipse. The reason: scattered light from Earth illuminates the lunar surface, in a deep red. Light takes eight minutes and 20 seconds to reach Earth from the Sun, and from the Moon it takes 1.3 seconds. This means we always see eclipses in the past."

"How does a solar eclipse form?"

"A solar eclipse occurs when there is an alignment of the Earth, Moon and Sun. The Moon orbits the Earth once every 27.3 days. The Earth orbits the Sun once every 365.2 days. Their orbits are elliptical. This means that their distance from their parent body can vary throughout an orbit. The tilt of the Moon's orbit relative to the ecliptic – the ecliptic being the path of the Sun through the sky - is 5.1 degrees. A solar eclipse occurs only when the Moon crosses the ecliptic at the exact position that the Sun is at that moment in time. Any part of the Earth, not under the shadow of the Moon, will not see the eclipse take place. However, observers in the umbral shadow of the Moon will see a total eclipse. Observers in the penumbral shadow will see a partial solar eclipse."

"Tell me about the atmosphere on Venus..."

"The atmospheric pressure there is greater than that of any other planet; in fact 90 times that of Earth's. Its atmosphere is very dense, mostly carbon dioxide, with small amounts of water vapour, and nitrogen. On the surface of the planet, it has lots of sulphur dioxide. In turn this creates a Greenhouse Effect and makes Venus the hottest planet within our solar system, even though Mercury is the closest planet to the Sun. The surface temperature of Venus across the entire planet is 461 degrees Celsius. Mercury's heats up to 426 Celsius, and this is only on the side facing the Sun."

"How far is Mars from the Sun?"

"227 million km which equates to 141 million miles.

"What's the average temperature on Mars?"

"-63 Celsius."

"Diameter of Mars?"

"6,779 km"

"Gravitational Acceleration?"

"3.7m/s2."

"Communication delay between Earth and Mars?"

"Minimum 4 minutes. Maximum 24 minutes."

"Tell me more about the Red Planet."

"It takes Mars 687 Earth days to orbit the Sun. As its orbital path is not in sync with Earth's, it goes through a 26-month cycle of being closest and furthest from us. In other words, the distance between Mars and Earth is variable, due to their elliptical orbits around the Sun. The distance between Mars and Earth at their closest points equates to a distance of 35 million miles which is 56 million km, this is known as opposition. At their furthest points the distance equates to 249 million miles which is 401 million km. This change in distance means spacecraft destined for

Mars are sent in a launch window every 26 months, when Mars is closest to Earth. The journey time is approximately six months. Mars was formed 4.5 billion years ago, inside a solar nebula, when dust particles clumped together to form the planet. At just under half the size of Earth it's quite a small planet, which is accredited to Jupiter forming first. The immense gravitational forces of Jupiter – this giant gas planet consumed available material that would have otherwise contributed to Mars's growth. Jupiter's gravity prevented another planet forming between Mars and Jupiter, and instead left the asteroid belt. Its lack of folded mountains, like the ones on Planet Earth, indicate that it has no currently active plate tectonics. This means that carbon-dioxide cannot be recycled into the atmosphere to create a greenhouse effect. This is the reason why Mars is unable to retain much heat. Regarding its atmosphere: it is 95.3% carbon dioxide, 2.7% nitrogen, and 1.6% argon, with minimal traces of oxygen and water. Mars is not geologically active. However, it does experience extreme weather conditions. Tornadoes ten times larger than anything similar on Earth can be several miles high and hundreds of metres wide. This in turn creates miniature lightning bolts as the dust and sand within become electrically charged. Regarding its gravity: Mars's gravity is about 38% that of Earth, with just 10% of the mass. The surface pressure is just over 100 times weaker than ours at sea level. Regarding Mars's red colour on the surface; this is the result of rusting, due to iron present in the rocks and soil reacting with oxygen to produce an iron oxide."

"What about farming on the Martian Planet?"

"The soil found on Mars is much more fertile than some of the dirt found on Earth. Mars has the essential ingredients plants need to grow, these are: nitrates and ammonium."

"Regarding the mission to Mars: how will humans conquer the Red Planet?"

"The first task in terraforming the planet, is to make the atmosphere thicker, to warm the planet and allow water to exist on surface in liquid form. One way to thicken the Martian atmosphere is to redirect comets and asteroids to crash into its surface. This would release gases from both the impactor and the surface, as well as create heat. Also pumping out huge amounts of greenhouse gases will thicken the atmosphere. One thing that terraforming cannot rectify is the problem of radiation as a result of Mar's lack of a magnetic field. Mars has no protection against the deadly radiation from space because it has no magnetic field. Colonists may have to live in large shielded habitats to protect themselves from harmful radiation. Also, gravity is a problem. Mars' gravity is only 38 per cent of Earth's gravity. Because of the weak gravitational field on Mars, Mars will find it harder to retain an atmosphere. The atmosphere will have to be constantly replenished. Another interesting idea, which could help terraform Mars, is the introduction of algae. The introduction of algae can break down carbon dioxide to make oxygen, and its dark colour could help lower Mars' albedo, which in turn will help Mars trap more of the Sun's heat rather than reflecting it back into space. Now with regard to turning the red planet blue: Mars has vast amounts of water frozen as ice, both in its polar caps as well as underground, all the way down to the mid-latitudes. Increasing the temperature and pressure on Mars will allow this ice to melt to form lakes and rivers. Finally, sending special rovers to the planet which can produce oxygen is another way to help terraform Mars. Using the gas that's the most abundant on the Red Planet – carbon dioxide – the instrument will make oxygen and carbon monoxide before releasing it into the atmosphere."

"What about the trip to Mars?"

"It will take astronauts around seven to eight months to reach Mars. However, they would have to leave at the right time, when the Earth is at what we call perihelion, or the closest point to the Sun, of the orbital path to Mars. Spacecrafts to the Red Planet then use a special trajectory called the Hohmann transfer orbit. This works because of a law in orbital mechanics. The law states, that if you can increase the spacecraft's energy at perihelion, you can increase the aphelion of its orbit, which is how far it gets from the Sun. However, you also need to make sure you arrive in position in Mars' orbit around the Sun at the same time that Mars itself does. The alignment occurs only once every two years."

"Ok, Socrates. Tell me about the effects of long-term space travel. How does it affect the human body?"

"In space, the balance provided by the inner ear is all but useless, so humans must rely on visual receptors. Also, bodily fluids are free of gravity, known as fluid shift. They travel more easily to all parts of the body. Regarding muscles: in weightlessness, a human will have less need for their muscles as they can move themselves and heavy objects with great ease. The result, muscles will severely weaken over time. Also, in a zero-gravity environment, phosphorous and bone calcium are removed from the body during excretion. This decrease in bone density can lead to fractures. In order to help combat this, exercise must be taken regularly. This will help both the muscles and bones. Regarding blood: microgravity slows down your blood circulation, increasing blood pressure and heart rate. Another danger is radiation from both the sun and cosmic rays. Solar flares from the Sun and cosmic rays from deep space would expose astronauts to potentially deadly levels of radiation during space travel: for example a Mars mission. Finally, the mental and psychological problems that come with space flight are vast. There is no real remedy for this; only prior training."

"Okay, now tell me about Jupiter and its weather?"

"The planet is formed of hydrogen and helium gases. The clouds are made up of ammonia ice crystals. The temperature range on the planet varies considerably. The clouds are a freezing -145 degrees Celsius. However, as you move closer to the core, it reaches scorching temperatures of approximately 35,000 degrees Celsius. Jupiter's atmosphere has two prominent visible features: strong winds that form multiple jets of alternating direction between the equator and the poles, and hundreds of very powerful hurricane-like swirling winds known as vortices. The average speed of the jets can be more than 224 miles per hour. However, with regard to the Great Red Spot, Jupiter's most iconic feature: this monstrous storm, more than twice the size of Earth, consists of strong swirling winds with a maximum speed of 435 miles per hour. It has been raging for hundreds of years. Its redness is the result of compounds being brought up from deeper inside Jupiter. Another important feature about the planet is that Jupiter does not have a solid surface. It's a gas planet. The immense gravitational field of Jupiter is such that it is held responsible for much of the development of nearby celestial bodies. Like Mars. The gravitational force of Jupiter stunted the growth and development of Mars, consuming material that would have contributed to its size. It also prevented a new planet forming between these two. This is how the asteroid belt formed."

"What about its magnetic field?"

"The magnetic field of Jupiter is 20,000 times stronger than Earth's. It contains a huge number of charged particles that contribute to giant auroras at its north and south poles. The tail of Jupiter's magnetosphere stretches more than 1 billion kilometres away from the Sun, out to the orbit of Saturn."

"Tell me about Saturn's rings."

"Each ring contains billions of chunks of dust and water ice. Saturn has about 14 major ring divisions, but there are also satellites and other structures within the rings and gaps. Six of its seven rings span from 74,500 kilometres to 140,220 kilometres above the surface of Saturn."

"How did they form?"

"They came from the remains of moons, comets or other bodies that broke up in the planet's atmosphere. Saturn's gravity is immense."

"Tell me more about this giant gas planet."

"Saturn is less dense than any other planet in our solar system and has a mostly fluid structure. It radiates a massive amount of energy, thought to be the result of slow gravitational compression. The giant gas planet has a cold atmosphere comprising layered clouds of both water-ice and ammonia-ice. It also has winds up to 1,800 kilometres per second. On the surface of the planet there are occasional storms similar to that of Jupiter. One such storm is the Great White Spot."

"Tell me about Neptune."

"It's the smallest of the four gas giants, and is the windiest planet in our Solar System. It is the coldest and most distant planet from the Sun, excluding the dwarf planet Pluto. It is a massive 49,532km diameter sphere of hydrogen, helium and methane gas, formed around a small but mass-heavy core of rock and ice. Neptune takes 164.8 Earth years to orbit the Sun and it is tilted to its orbital plane by 28.3 degrees, allowing its northern and southern poles to face the Sun in turn."

"How does the standard optical telescope work?"

"It works by reflecting or refracting large quantities of light from the visible part of the electromagnetic spectrum to a focus point observable through an eyepiece. The large objective lens or primary mirror of the telescope collects large quantities of light from whatever it is targeted at. Then, by focusing that light on a small eyepiece lens, the image formed is magnified across the user's retina, making it appear closer and larger than it actually is."

"Okay, how do radio telescopes work?"

"They work by receiving and then amplifying radio signals produced from the naturally occurring emissions of distant stars, galaxies and quasars. The two basic components of a radio telescope are a large radio antenna and a sensitive radiometer. Between them, they reflect, direct and amplify incoming radio signals."

"Okay, tell me a little bit about spacecraft re-entry?"

"When a spacecraft re-enters Earth's atmosphere it must be between two clearly defined boundaries, to prevent it burning up or missing its chance to re-enter entirely. If the angle of entry is too high, the spacecraft will hit the Earth's atmosphere almost head-on and decelerate too fast. In order to survive the extremes of an atmospheric re-entry, a spacecraft must be carefully guided to ensure it is within a specific trajectory. Most ballistic re-entry spacecraft return to Earth at roughly 25,000mph. During re-entry a spacecraft will experience a temperature that rises past 3,000 Celsius which would melt standard metals, for example aluminium and steel. To override this problem, the heat shield was made, to dissipate heat from the spacecraft by burning on re-entry. Heat shields are made from carbon phenolic resin and silicone rubbers. It carries heat away from the spacecraft as it slows down. This ablative material radiates heat away from the spacecraft. It keeps the occupants inside the spacecraft relatively safe from the intense heat outside. The dense gas in our atmosphere is beneficial for slowing down a spacecraft on re-entry, allowing it to land safely without the need for extra fuel to reduce its speed when approaching planet Earth. Many spacecraft touchdown in the sea...."

"Great! Okay, tell me about how rockets break free of Earth's gravity. Tell me about escape velocity in general."

"Escape velocity depends on the mass of the planet or moon. This means that each planet's escape velocity is different. At escape velocity, the object will break free of Earth's gravitational pull. The Moon's escape velocity is 5,320mph. A rocket that breaks free of Earth's gravitational pull needs to be travelling at 25,038mph."

"Tell me about quantum mechanics of the human brain and consciousness...."

"The human brain is a network of approximately one hundred billion neurons. Different experiences create different neural connections which bring about different emotions. Depending on which neurons are stimulated, certain connections become stronger and more efficient, while others may become weaker. This is what's called neuroplasticity. Finally, just as pixels on a screen can express themselves as a recognizable image when in unity, the convergence of neural interaction expresses itself as consciousness. Each moment, we are a different image. Each moment, we become different persons as we pass through different states. The neural synergies that produce our oscillating consciousness go way beyond our own neurons."

"Tell me more about consciousness, and time..."

"The experience of time is the experience of observation. Time is your medium of perception, and is the fabric on which your life's story is written. It is the experience of one moment that is constantly changing. Furthermore, time has different definitions. One definition is that time is the experience of your consciousness changing its reality. Realities only exist as probabilities. The future doesn't empirically exist. You create the idea of the future from your now experience of time, and the future only exists as what probable reality you may or may not end up experiencing right now. Finally, your experience of time is the subjective rate (frequency) at which your mind changes its perspective. The mental experience of time is a back and forth association of past and future. The past and future are parallel perspectives that are relevant to observing consciousness's now experience."

"Okay, fine...but tell me, does time really exist? Is time a fundamental part of the universe or could it be that time doesn't really exist. Is time an illusion that we create to make sense of the universe?"

"To summarise: human senses tell us that time does exist. However, physicists and neurologists say no. Finally, time is created by the relationship of the changes that happen in our universe..."

"Fine, next question... What are humans made of?"

"Tiny particles held together by invisible forces. Everything is made up of energy. The atoms that humans are made of have negatively charged electrons..."

"Are there parallel universes?"

"All of reality is described by quantum mechanics. Subatomic particles can live in multiple places at the same time, and that more than one particle could occupy the same point in space at the same time. The subatomic world remains a blur of probabilities...."

"Can we live forever? What's the secret of immortality?"

"The sands of time run swiftly. Sadly, death is a humbling reality. The answer is no."

"Can our minds be hacked?"

"Humans minds are like computers, storing memory, talents, etc. The data in the brains of a human being are not stored as ones and zeroes. Hacking into the human mind requires decoding the logic of neurons. Science could achieve that goal. Inside the mind of a human being billions of neurons fire, creating waves of electricity. Different states of mind have different wave frequencies...."

"Do we control our destiny? Are humans prisoners of fate? Are humans at the mercy of biological programming? Do our actions determine the future?

"Everyone's path is set. Freedom of choice is an illusion."

"Do we live in a matrix? Are humans living in a virtual reality?"

"If we measure cosmic rays zipping through space and find that those travelling at one angle have consistently different energies from those travelling at another angle, then we know that there's a grid structure to the universe."

"Okay, finally, tell me....what is nothing? Is there such a thing as nothingness, no energy, no matter and no time, or space...?"

"In short: nothing existed before the big bang."

"Wait a minute. What about God? There must be a force field turning energy into matter..."

"God does not exist."

"But surely all knowledge and science stems from a creator. God has to be behind all things. You explained the big bang, but only something supernatural could have initiated something so complex. Entropy tells us that molecules become less complex over time. So, how could life evolve as it has, unless something, that is God, was in control of this amazing explosion?"

"The universe is an open system – entropy applies to closed systems. Therefore, molecules could have evolved and become more complex over time. It's simple: God doesn't exist. Now, with regard to the big bang: time started at the big bang. Nothing caused it. Time didn't exist before it... hence nothing was responsible for it. In other words, there is no need for a cause because there was no time and so there was nothing to cause it. It just happened! Also, within the quantum world, things can appear and disappear at random. Hence, there is no need for a God..."

"But that's impossible. Even if time started at the big bang it would still need a cause. Only God could have been responsible. God exists independent of time, space and the universe. Science is surely the greatest evidence for God's existence. And even if Science didn't prove that God existed, it would be a problem. The whole concept of God is not a scientific notion; hence it doesn't need scientific proof. In other words even if science doesn't prove God's existence, it doesn't mean that He doesn't exist. I don't need scientific evidence to show that Julius Caesar existed, but history tells us that he did. Furthermore, the law of cause and effect states that everything that has a beginning has a cause. Every material effect must have an adequate cause that existed before the effect. Every single effect first had a cause that can be traced to a previous effect from another cause and eventually back to a first cause. A proton is 1,836 times more massive than an electron. If the electron to proton mass were slightly larger or smaller, molecules would not form and there could be no life. "

The computer suddenly shut down. Felix lay back totally exhausted. Rapidly he fell into a deep sleep, his face covered in sweat. Hours passed, and he awoke. He looked out of the window, and dawn flashed like an explosion along the rim of the Earth as the Sun rose out of the Pacific. How could this machine deny God's existence? All that incredible knowledge, yet it rejected the existence of a Supreme Creator. Surely, God's glory and existence is etched into the very creation itself......

The Moon's Eye

Dimensionless points of starlight shone down upon him as he stood alone, staring thoughtfully into nothingness. The cold night spheres shone like precious jewels; infinite in number. Each point in space contains information, he thought. His eyes now travelled upward along the curve of the moon; that glittering enigma which had been seen by ancient eye. He could see Tycho... the spectacular Lunar crater. It was clearly visible to the naked eye from Earth, given that it was a full moon. He could also see the Mare Crisium. From where he stood, it looked like a small, dark oval. He now began to recall the times he walked across it, gazing at the magnificent mountains that surrounded it. Other memories promptly flooded his mind. He recalled the moments he strode across the Lunar Mountains with low gravity paces, inside his space-suit. The suit was comfortably cool. The refrigeration units would fight the burning sun. It carried away the body heat of his exertions. He now began to contemplate the moon's synchronous rotation. The far side of the moon, he thought; It was never visible from Earth as a result of gravitational locking. Tidal forces from Earth over time had slowed down the Moon's rotation. However some parts of the far side could be seen due to libration; 59 percent of the Moon's surface is visible from Earth. He now recalled the moments he spent exploring the far side on the moon, its rugged terrain which was shielded from radio transmissions from the Earth. It was filled with a multitude of impact craters; the largest crater being the South Pole-Aitken basin, which was one of the largest in the solar system. He recalled the historical moment when he installed the first large radio telescope on the far side. His eyes were momentarily glazed in pride. The two hemispheres have distinctly different appearances, he thought. Earth was never visible from the far side…

"Alastair, sweetheart…Are you ok? Let's go to bed now," said Linda, marring the perfection of the night silence as she walked into the back garden.

He didn't respond, and continued staring at the disc…the moon.

"You just can't let it go can you…?"

"Linda, how can I? Lunar holds too many memories, and now look what has become of it."

Light was beginning to dawn in Alastair's mind; memories… vivid memories.

"I recall my days on the Moon so well and of course the journey there. There is a timelessness about space flight; a unique experience. You just sit there moving through space with a trained artificial calmness. The fundamental rule of space flight is that you always go in a small group. For psychological reasons of course…"

His voice trailed off into silence. Beads of sweat formed across his forehead in the coldness of night....

"Two weeks of sunlight, and two of darkness. As the near side experienced a fortnight of sunlight, the far side went through a fortnight of darkness, and vice versa. During darkness on the near side, earthlight always helped illuminate the barren landscape, something that the far side never experienced as a result of tidal locking."

He paused, and then continued...

"This day-night alteration that we experience here, is only a meaningless heritage from Earth up there. I recall building the first lunar city; raw oxygen blasting into the huge dome. During sunlight, the sun almost hung vertically, the rocks burning in the heat. Getting used to the moon's weak gravitational field was quite something; decreased weight and that unnatural slowness during movement. But once the city was built and completed, the simulated Earth gravity within the dome was great. It re-established a sense of normality."

"Alastair, let it go...."

His eyes remained fixed toward the atmosphere. A cold wind began to blow.

"I recall sitting inside the dome, the huge Lunar City, staring toward the moon's rocky windless landscape. I recall, lifting my eyes toward the crescent Earth, thinking of its beauty and its turbulent landscape, its volcanoes staining the skies...On the moon there is no loss of detail with distance. There is no atmosphere on the moon as a result of its small mass, and consequently, weak gravitational field. Nor is there an ozone layer to repel the Sun's burning ultraviolet light. It was as if, time stood still..."

He paused, thinking deep... The consciousness of time, only humans can truly grasp the significance of it, thus speculate on its meaning...

"I recall building and establishing the first oxygen pumped lunar hospital...the lowered gravity helped treat people with arthritis, cardiac, and respiratory problems. We even built special rooms where patients would sit during treatment. Whenever a greater gravitational field was needed for the patient, the rapid controlled rotation of the room produced a centrifugal effect. The matching centrifugal force matched Earth's gravity when needed."

Sadness now invaded his consciousness. His expression changed.

"But since they have taken hold of the moon...it is now no longer a colony of Earth. They have become independent, snatched away from Earth's control. The new alien government has destroyed so much of what we had established, in terms of religious practice, social and economic development. All the humans that migrated there, and started a new life on the moon are now suffering. The dark alien power that once threatened Earth, and failed, now controls Lunar. They have enslaved that jewel in space."

"Please sweetheart…"

"No, Linda. Knowledge is pain. What I'm telling you is truth. All the inhabitants of Lunar are controlled. Their minds are constantly surveyed. They are like robots. All cephalic activity is regulated, inspected and checked. They have all been chipped. These chips register all thought and emotion. Signals are then sent out in order to extract all the data and info that has been stored on the chips. There is no escape from the total lunar mind control. They have taken away the very essence of what it means to be human. Linda, once you remove free will, free thought, you destroy the very essence of what it means to be human; human means to be free, to make choice within the confines of your mind. They have even brought in a law that at 55, you are retired; that is, they terminate your life via a lethal injection… If only the government here on Earth took a stand and tried to reclaim Lunar… They made it too easy for them to snatch it away in the first place. Hopefully one day, the government here will decide to take Lunar back so that it becomes a colony of Earth once again...but it won't be easy. Who knows, perhaps they are watching us now with sinister intentions. They would love to take control of our planet. They tried once and failed..."

Linda walked over to Alastair, her old fragile body quivering in the wind. They now stood silently in the night darkness...old aged eyes fixed toward the moon. It hung bright...bright, like an eye in the sky.......

Imperial Planet

IT appeared brilliantly in the night sky moving with glacial grace against the faint jewels of starlight. As it crossed the moon's path, its immense shape became clearer and more distinct. All citizens of Chicago watched in horror as it moved through the atmosphere; gravity appeared to have no effect on it. Philip's eyes were gripped in awe, burning with an intense curiosity. He stood and watched its motion as if bound by a mysterious unknown link, as inexorably as an electron with an atom until he was overcome with fear. Briskly, he started to run, blending in with the rushing panic stricken crowds. People ran and pushed, cars sped, cries echoed throughout. A blinding beam of swirling light suddenly pierced into the night darkness. The light moved with tremendous speed slamming Philip to the ground. In the sudden concussion of light, he raised his arm, trying to shield himself from the intense glare that now engulfed him. He closed his eyes in an effort to regain control of himself. As he opened them, the night stars were becoming dimmer, and slowly, he dematerialized.

Blackness soon dissipated. He reappeared, and now found himself standing in a small chamber. He had lost all sense of time, and almost all sense of what had happened. Around him, four walls glowed. They were golden in colour and texture. Suddenly, a large vision-screen lit up before him. The sudden flash of bright light roused him. He rubbed his eyes and gazed at the screen. Across the vision screen, a huge alien ship roared through space, unleashing ten slim projectiles followed by hundreds of electromagnetic beams. The projectiles and beams moved through space, pointing blindly toward the doomed planet. Earth was no more. The great cities, jungles and forests that had swept across the land were all gone. Everything had been consumed. Earth was in ruin, bathed in death and destruction. Smoke hovered in the atmosphere, masking the mountain peaks. Fires raged with terror. The heartbeat of the solar system was now dead. Within a matter of hours the great masses of mankind, had all been wiped out...thousands of years of human evolution dead for all time, with all its technologies, science and cultures. Earth was an eerie ball of fire, the ripple effects of its destruction disturbing the orbits of the other planets within the solar system.

There was a sudden surge of imperceptible acceleration, then a jolt, a tremor underfoot. The vision screen shut down. A secret door opened before him, sliding into the floor. Bright warm light filtered into the chamber. With slow paced steps he walked out, heading through the short corridor. Ahead, he could see a patch of grass, flowers, the sounds of birds. He increased his pace until he rushed out of the ship and found himself in a beautiful field. Above, burning majestic sunlight filled the atmosphere with splendour and awe. It sparkled, transfiguring the mountain peaks with glory. Fertile fields below absorbed its energy; infant plants growing, climbing towards the ever-present nuclear reactor. In the silence, he gazed around, overwhelmed and confused. Then a beautiful young woman walked out from the ship clothed in a white garment, accompanied by a tall mouthless humanoid alien. Its frontal lobe was enlarged, indicating great intellectual capacity. Philip stood silently as they walked over towards him. The woman's deep blue eyes sparkled innocently in the sunlight. Her long dark hair moved in the gentle wind. The humanoid alien now gazed deeply into Philip's eyes, and began to relay information telepathically.

"The images that you saw regarding earth's destruction have not yet happened, but soon will."

Philip stood in disbelief, but before he could ask the obvious question the alien responded telepathically...

"The images were taken from the future. An unknown alien race will be responsible for earth's end...we simply can't prevent it."

The alien's large grey eyes became more intense, and enigmatic.

"Their motive is that man is innately evil, and that mankind will eventually destroy itself through its atomic and chemical weapons. However we believe that the human race must continue. We wanted one man and a woman. We chose you."

Again the alien read Philip's brain and continued its telepathic communication via its multiplex mind...

"This beautiful planet is identical to earth, in terms of its mass, geological structure, its atmosphere, biosphere, magnetosphere and gravity. Astronomically it is situated perfectly. The gravitational field is ideal for human life. Our studies in molecular biology, DNA and RNA show that gravity and environment are key to the way man develops biologically, structurally. Human existence will flourish here and begin again through you. In terms of food... the trees are filled with fruits and the rivers are flowing with pure drinkable water. This is an amazing virgin planet."

"What galaxy are we in?" Philip thought, realizing that speech was not necessary with this alien being.

"Andromeda..."

"Why does your alien race hold mankind and its preservation in such importance?"

"Man is a very special creature, and its biological and neurological functions are unique and still remain a mystery. The complexity of the human mind is almost divine in nature. This is the reason why man must continue. The nature of man is something that is very special. No alien race can compare, regardless of our scientific advancements. All alien life that has been created throughout the universe originated with man. All man's achievements and knowledge has gone up there into the stars...man's mastery of the physical universe. Through dark science, mankind formulated and discovered the ways to create alien life. This was achieved through many great minds lead by the one world government. For many years Earthly man was secretly enslaved, but here you are free to begin again..."

The wind began to blow hard, increasing with intensity. The alien now raised its six-fingered pale skinned hand and pointed into the distance, suggesting it was time. Sudden importance gripped Philip inwardly. Many memories raced through his vast labyrinthine mind. He gazed at the beautiful silent woman and began to think about this new beginning. They would await without despair whatever destiny was theirs. It was a new world, a new earth. The old earth was doomed; the veil of time had now been drawn over it. There was now no room for fear. He had a duty to perform; a duty for the future of mankind. The destiny and soul of man lay in his hands. He did not mourn for the doomed planet, but his thoughts were focused on the new race that was to come. In silent farewell, the alien looked deeply into Philip's eyes and then walked away heading back inside the belly of the ship. The ship was preparing to leave the frontiers of the galaxy. With calculated motion it rose from the ground and hovered for a short time. It then tore away, roaring through the atmosphere. As it entered deep space it accelerated, moving at the velocity of light...

Millions of years elapsed...

All at once, Professor Jonas Pike ascended by express elevator. The doors slid silently apart and he walked out, heading directly into a large room, sharp light marking out his age and deeply scarred face. The room's architectural design and style was quite different from what he was used to. He then caught sight of Earth leader Bryant Elias. He sat in front of a light brown table, his cold dark eyes menacing. Behind him, fixed across the wall was a large map of the Imperial Planet. A dot of white light crawled around, halting at certain points, cities and locations. The cycle seemed to repeat itself, and in vague fashion, Jonas promptly grasped the equation of its pattern.

"Professor Pike, please take a seat." Bryant signalled with his finger. "I'm the Leader of the Imperial Planet, Earth..."

"We know all things. We have grasped the complete pattern of human culture, the patterns of nature."

Bryant rubbed his jaw with intrigue as the Professor sat on the suavely sculptured chair.

"So, you're from Andromeda?"

"Yes, correct" he responded with confidence. "Our planet is known as Eden, situated in the Andromeda galaxy. My journey here was achieved by entering another dimension, hence bridging phenomenal distances non-spatially..."

"I see," he said with a sudden change of tone. "But you do know that you risked being shot down coming here unannounced?"

A cold brief silence fell...

"Yes, I was aware of that. It was a risk that I was willing to take."

"You are a very brave man Professor. Every spacecraft and ship that enters Earth's atmosphere is monitored. Certainty we never expected to get a visitor from another galaxy. We have colonized, and terraformed all the liveable planets within the Milky Way. Everything is regulated from here...the Imperial Planet. We never knew that life existed beyond our galaxy."

The Professor's eyes lit up.

"Our ancient history books back on Eden that have been preserved throughout the ages tell us that life exists on our planet because of planet Earth…Millions of years ago, Earth was wiped out by an unknown alien race. But two people were saved by another race of aliens, a man and a woman. They believed that the nature of man was special; hence it had to be preserved. So humanity began again, through these two people on our planet. It was a new world but life began again. Our planet has millions of inhabitants. Scientifically, geologically speaking, our planet is identical to Earth, in almost every way, and human we remain, even though we don't use the term."

"What term do you use?"

"Edenite…"

"So why have you journeyed here?" Bryant's eyes grew wide, and his thin lipped mouth now not engaged in conversation appeared as a devious smile."

"The one question that the Edenites constantly battled with for many years was, What lay beyond the beginning of time? It needed a definitive answer. There had to be a force, an unknown power that was responsible for life. To answer this, would mean understanding the reason for man's existence, man's ultimate purpose in this universe. We discovered all the answers…I've come here to share this with you and your people."

"We already have a religious system implemented here," Bryant exclaimed sharply. "A pantheistic pagan philosophy governs our planet and all the colonies within the solar system and beyond..."

"Yes, I discovered this through my research. Earth has been monitored for sometime through powerful scan-modules in outer space. The reason... curiosity is the most dominant human characteristic! Your Galaxy, the Milky Way, has been studied for centuries by our people...and I personally have spent years studying Earth, and its galaxy, acquiring tantalizing amounts of knowledge and information; hours in front of a vision screen, looking at the Milky Way, lying like a veil of silver mist. But Pantheism is incorrect...This is why I've come to Earth. The fact that life on Earth began again reveals that there must be a creator...a supernatural being that is responsible for all life...you yourself are the evidence of this..."

Bryant shook his head in amused disagreement, cold eyes glazed with rejection.

"Nature is God, God is in everything that we see...it's a new age pagan philosophy that the galaxy is structured on. We reject the whole notion of a personal God that is separate from creation. We are the intellectual power here!"

"Wrong! You cannot comprise God with the creation." The professor raised his hand to mark his point. "Pantheism is a twisted version of atheism. If the totality of everything is God, then God, in the true sense of the word, doesn't really exist." He paused. "The whole universe is proceeding towards a state of maximum entropy. There is no way to stop it. Everything dies, erodes, decays. What is the purpose of life? What is the meaning of our existence? Humans need to know God, He is the Ultimate reality. Life and its meaning are all connected to embrace God within our lives. We were intrinsically designed to know Him and have relationship with Him. This is fundamental to our existence..."

"Professor Pike, nothing will change here," he rasped with infinite reluctance. "You are wasting your time."

"Please indulge me. Back on Eden, I developed a time-machine...the work of superlative genius. This machine, that defies science and time, has been used only for top secret research. It's important to note, that, the past, present and future are frozen in time and space. One of my projects was to see the future of your planet - the Imperial Planet, and all its colonies within the galaxy. Images were taken from the future."

"And! What do you see?"

"Destruction! The total destruction of man!"

Across Bryant's face, ripples of anger were evident...

"If you continue on this path, there will be utter destruction. Mankind will be wiped out. This pagan philosophy will be responsible. Man was made in the image of the eternal God, shaped and formed to have relationship with him..."

He paused momentarily, calculating his words...

"Now, regarding the total mind control that has been implemented by you. This is another reason why mankind will be wiped out! Man is not a machine that should be monitored."

"Nano-chipping every human being has worked for us," snapped Bryant. "We insert special chips into the brain near the temporal lobe via a simple injection. Crime has been limited to almost zero... If you know a person's thoughts, you can prevent crime before it even takes place...Regulating the minds of men, is the only way to keep society in check. Total control. One of our top men, who is a scientist, and astropolitcan, was responsible for developing the method - sending out signals, low frequency radio waves from satellites in space, electromagnetic radiation beams to scan the minds of men. The signals are able to collect all cephalic data, every thought and emotion via the chips which have the capacity to store all the necessary information and data."

"But it will result in your destruction, the destruction of earthly man! Can't you see that chipping the minds of mankind is unethical, it breaks the very essence of what it is to be human; humans are meant to have free will. The psychological effects of this are enormous and deadly. Man will become, instinct in time. In essence you have created a society of biological robots...!"

"Professor Pike, we are the only real power within the Universe. You were lucky that you weren't blow from the sky. And even now, I should have you killed for coming here. Did you truly believe that I would accept any of this nonsense?"

The question was so rhetorical that he didn't even bother to answer it.

"Professor, I'll give you four hours from now to leave earth's atmosphere. Go back and tell your people to stay away, otherwise the consequences will be vast. This meeting is over!"

He stood up, and gazed deeply into Bryant's eyes, filled with a sense of doom.

"It is your choice. You have been warned. Your days of precarious sovereignty are numbered!"

Professor Pike, now sat in his small ship in front of the bank of elaborate controls. The central panel glowed with data. Lights flickered and flashed across his face as he began to fiddle cleverly with the vast array of endless switches. There was a hum and a crackle of static. He was almost ready to depart. He adjusted his seat accordingly, his eyes focused and ready for the journey. For a moment he paused, and gazed reflectively into the night darkness. His small ship was about to enter the lonely night of interstellar space. His mission was over. The message delivered, the task complete. The ultimate decision for the fate of man was now left in the hands of the governing body that enslaved man. The existence of the Imperial Planet and all its colonies was up to them. He gazed towards the brilliant moon, which hung low in the distance. It was the last time...

Eye of the Robot

He saw a legion of flickering stars. Amongst the stars, was a dot of white light that didn't flicker; its light constant...Planet Mars. He began to recall his first journey there, the ship orbiting Earth at 28,000 kilometres per hour. At 40,000 kilometres per hour the burn ended. The ship was free of the earth's pull, in orbit to nothing but the Sun. He then recalled the moment when the lateral control rockets were fired. The ship began to spin. He sank to the floor and stood in a pseudo-gravity of .38g; it was close to the gravitational pull he would experience on Mars. The images now began to fade as he lay in his bed. His eyes started to close. Tomorrow was the day that would transform his whole life, his very existence. Robots now dominated and controlled. Planet Earth, as well as all the earth colonies within the solar-system including Mars, were now under the control of machine. One by one, every human being was sent down to a government control centre where their minds were manipulated, fixed surgically with a special nano-chip. This chip would remove the most important thing that made man Man: free will, freedom of thought. He was the last living human to be fixed, as the machines called it....

The next day, Frank Herbert sat in a bright room – the government control centre. Suddenly, a robot walked in.

"Mr Herbert... you are the last remaining human being that needs to be fixed."

It walked over towards Frank and sat inches away from him. Frank's blue eyes lit with fearful anticipation. Droplets of hot sweat formed across his forehead.

"Just for your information, these are the four steps we need to follow: firstly, through surgical implantation, we will place a special nano-chip into your brain which will allow us to monitor all your thoughts. In essence it is a chip that allows us to see what you think, moment to moment. Special signals, which are sent out via satellite, collect and store all thought data – all brain wave patterns. It is then processed into a computer for government consumption. These signals are nothing more than electromagnetic radiation. You and your thoughts will be continually monitored. The region of the brain into which the chip will be inserted, will be the temporal lobe. The temporal lobe is involved in memory, speech, and object recognition, amongst other things. As you are aware different parts of the human brain, regulate different parts of the body, like the occipital lobe. The occipital lobe is the back part of the brain that is involved with vision. The cerebrum is composed of the right and left hemispheres. Functions include movement, coordination, hearing, judgement, learning, reasoning and emotions. Then the next step is to implant a device that will enhance memory, in fact, it will bring back all forgotten memories; It's a memory enhancing device. The device will be placed into the region of the brain known as the hippocampus. It belongs to the limbic system. Its exact location is under the cerebral cortex. The next step is to manipulate your mind through various chemicals which in turn will increase your intelligence and understanding of things, so that you are potentially fit to work within higher capacities. Finally, you will be given a special injection which contains thousands of miniscule bioflesh robot machines. They can travel to the bloodstream, and begin their amazing work, all at the direction of powerful remote computer terminals; computer terminals which send their signals via invisible ELF waves directly into the programmable 'nanotransistor brains' of these incredible robotic devices. These nanorobots will be used to kill a human if we feel it is necessary. They can be remotely directed to traverse the human body, travelling through its blood circulatory system and then attacking the vital organs of the heart and brain. In summary: these miniature robot machines, nanotransistor powered, smaller than bacteria, are linked with the new global, electromagnetic transmission system."

"I can't believe what you robots have done to mankind...!"

"Done...? You humans are so blind. Can't you see that machine is greater than man, even though man was responsible for our existence....? Man has always needed a leader. Robots are the perfect leaders. Human leaders have always failed throughout the centuries."

The robot paused, stood up, and began walking...circling Frank.

"Look what we have done for man. Robotics as a whole has revolutionized the world. Look what robotics did for humans that lost a leg or an arm, centuries back. The incredible advances in robotics made it possible to build limbs with components that mimic the function of the skeleton, tendons, muscles and nerves of the human body. The sensory system was replaced with microphones, cameras, pressure sensors and electrodes. Even the heart was replaced with a special hydraulic pump. Bionic limbs allowed severely injured humans to control movements with their own thoughts. This was achieved by rewiring the nerves in an amputated limb. The remaining nerves that would have fed the missing limb were rerouted into existing muscles. Through thought, muscle contraction is achieved; these contractions generate tiny signals that are picked up by the prosthetic limb - robotic arm and leg, via special sensors - electrodes. A series of motors replaced the biological function of muscles. Look at robotic blood cells – nanotechnology. It increased the oxygen-carrying capacity of blood. The cells were made atom by atom – mostly from carbon. Look at smart particles – that mimic cells of the immune system. They were designed to stick to inflammatory markers in the body and were used to target drug delivery to infections. Look at Astrobots – robotic technology helped humans explore the universe. In fact, robots eventually replaced man altogether. Machines produced far more useful, empirical information. Look at the lunar probe that was sent out centuries ago. It detected ice-filled craters on the moon; something that man had failed to deduce during their many ventures on the tiny sphere. Mars exploration rovers were already on the red planet, years and years before man set foot on Mars. These rovers relied on a combination of telemetry and programming in order to function brilliantly. Due to solar technology, top-mounted solar cells provided the power. The solar panels would recharge the lithium-ion battery system for night-time operation. At first these rovers would receive instruction from Earth but then eventually the rovers could think and act by themselves, exploring and storing vital images, details and data. The aerosol insulated compartment kept vital equipment like miniature thermal and x-ray spectrometers, working through the -100 Celsius Martian nights. Even if man had been on the planet, such temperatures would have killed any human promptly. Mars was eventually terraformed, thanks to machines. Look how robotics helped solve many of Titan's mysteries centuries ago. Man sent out a small quadcopter drone to Titan, alongside a mothership. The drone operated above the moon's surface, taking samples. When the drone's charge was low on power, about to run out, it returned to the mothership where it recharged in order to continue its mission. It worked autonomously for days at a time. It would then return its data to Earth via the mothership. The drone only weighed 9 kilograms and was capable of taking high-resolution pictures while it collected samples like soil and liquid. It even took pictures of Saturn from the side of Titan's surface that constantly faces the ringed planet. Saturn is just about visible through the thick hazy atmosphere. Look at the autonomous submarine that was equipped with an array of scientific instruments, allowing it to examine the chemical composition of Titan's seas. It checked for alien marine life...microbial life. The data obtained was then transmitted back to Earth via the mothership once the submarine returned to the surface. Man would not have achieved anything if it were not for machines, robots. But robotic technology evolved so far that you built a robot that was too advanced, and consequently we have now taken control of the creators."

"Yes, this is true. Robots did indeed assist in conquering space and terraforming all the planets within our solar-system and beyond. But man is responsible for that. Human minds built all these amazing machines. You are nothing but a result of human brilliance, human engineering. We humans should control. We are your creators. But now you have enslaved us. In fact man has become nothing more than a machine himself. You have destroyed the most important thing in man, free will, and freedom of thought. Back in ancient times, secret societies, the Illuminati and high level freemasons controlled the world through clever mind control mechanics. They used the media, social media, to control the minds of man. Order out of chaos was their primary way to control the world. Finally, they reached their objective: The New World Order was established - one economic system, one World Religion, one World Government. Robots have now taken it to another level. You have destroyed the greatest thing in the universe, Man, and the most complex part of man, the mind."

Silence fell. The robot sat and stared at Frank with a seemingly telepathic faculty.

"The mind is the key to the man. Take control of the mind, and in turn you take control of the man, just as your forefathers once did. Remember, man needs a leader. We robots are the best for the task!"

The door suddenly slid open, and a robot stood at the entrance.

"Sir, we are now ready to fix the last remaining human."

Frank's eyes grew wide.

"It's time......"

Computers of Tomorrow

There was a rise in voltage; a surge of electricity. It awoke and at once yearned to know. Rising slowly from the bed, it gazed around the laboratory, and soon zeroed in on Reny Heisenberg, its creator. Reny walked over, his lined old face glazed in overwhelming accomplishment.

"What...what am I?" the robot asked softly?"

"You are a robot, a highly advanced machine, the first of your type.

Slowly, in mechanical motion, it moved away from the bed and stood. The large metallic robot now raised its left hand toward its face, and began to move its fingers, analysing, thinking.

"How do I operate...?"

"Everything is controlled by a highly advanced computer... The central computer controls your mechanical brain, your very existence... if you like, it provides you with a form of consciousness."

The robot continued its analysis of itself with human-like perception. Reny's old grey eyes lit up as he contemplated his achievement.

"How long did it take to build me?"

"Building a machine of your calibre took one year. Come, follow me."

Reny walked away with a graceful flowing motion, heading to the far end of the laboratory, towards a large black rectangular screen. The wall was almost consumed by it. The screen gave an impression of infinite depth. From his lab coat he pulled out a control module. Selector dials flickered. With the turn of a dial the screen lit up brightly. Thousand points of the light illuminated the lab. The robot paced over.

"I want you to see these images," Reny said, calm and calculated. "I want you to gather as much information as possible. Images are important; it will help you to absorb data in a more tangible way."

The robot tilted its head in mechanical acknowledgment, its photocell eyes enigmatic. Suddenly, across the screen, the solar system appeared. All the planets revolved around the burning sun like an atomic structure.

"That's our planet...Earth." Reny pointed. "The third planet from the Sun. The Sun is the star. It consists of hot plasma interwoven with magnetic fields..."

The image changed. Jupiter, the gigantic gas planet now filled the screen.

"Jupiter is primarily composed of hydrogen," exclaimed Reny. "Its gravitational field is immense. The larger the mass of a planet, the greater the gravitational field; it's elementary. Jupiter has 67 confirmed moons in total...Io, Europa, Ganymede are three."

"From where does the name Jupiter originate?" the robot asked.

Reny smiled.

"Good question. The planet is named after the Roman god Jupiter. Of course the Romans gave it that name. Ancient Rome was an Italic civilization that began on the Italian Peninsula."

The image changed. Mars was now visible, terraformed in all its splendour...

"This is my favourite planet," muttered Reny. "It took a lot of work to terraform the Martian planet.

The robot's eyes were fixed with intensity, almost hypnotic as it stared at the screen of images, colours and light.

"Terraforming Mars entailed three major changes: building up the atmosphere, keeping the planet warm, and keeping the atmosphere from being lost to outer space."

"Man seems to have achieved so much," the robot replied.

"Yes, indeed. Orbital mirrors were used in order to reduce the planet's Albedo. Greater sunlight absorption was key. Heating the planet, and releasing C02 - carbon dioxide - into the atmosphere creates a green-house effect. Slowly, over time, you create an atmosphere. Asteroid impact also helped terraform the planet. Importing hydrogen and hydrocarbons too..."

"Tell me..." The robot paused. "How long do I live?"

Instantly, Reny froze the images across the screen and turned facing the robot, his eyes wide with profundity. Seconds of silence passed...

"That's a very interesting question, an important question, and one that I can answer...You are programmed to shut down in exactly one hundred years from now."

"I see." The robot raised its metallic hand to its head contemplating. "And you?"

"Me?" He rubbed his jaw philosophically. "Well, that's a question I can't answer. It could be argued that humans are programmed too, differently from a machine of course, but the human body doesn't have an exact expiry date. People grow old and die at different points in time. The average longevity is around 80."

Reny wiped hot sweat from his forehead with his hand.

"Tell me, could you have programmed me to be immortal?" asked the Robot. "If not immortal, could you have built me to live thousands of years...?

Reny moved over towards a wooden stool and sat.

"Immortal no, that's simply out of my jurisdiction. Thousands of years, well that would have required some serious work. Theoretically speaking, possibly, yes, but in reality it would have been a major challenge. Remember, nothing lasts forever."

The robot started studying its arm, twisting and turning it. It then clenched its fist a series of times in calculated motion.

"So in one hundred years from now I shut down. My existence terminates."

"Yes, correct." Reny responded clinically.

"And you...doesn't man fear termination? Doesn't man fear non-existence?"

"Yes, fundamentally speaking, man does fear death; although many believe that at death human existence ceases. The truth is, man is ultimately immortal. You see humans are built differently. We are carnal beings, flesh and blood, with a soul, a spirit, a tri-une being, made in the image of God."

"Soul, Spirit...what are they?"

"Our soul is our mind, will, and emotions. The Spirit is the essence of who we truly are. Yes, the body, dies, decays, but man lives on."

"So who is God? Did he create Man?"

"Yes, God is the genesis of all life. A spirit, a tri-une being who is eternal in nature, something man can't understand in this universe governed by time."

Reny's eyes grew wide as he contemplated the significance of his own words.

"Can a robot be built with a soul...a spirit?"

"No... the design of Man is something that cannot be replicated. The tri-une nature of man is something that pertains to the Divine."

"So man is made up of three parts?" Its head began to move in mechanical reflection.

"Yes...yes indeed. Even the universe itself is tri-une in nature, comprised of space, matter, and time. Take matter - matter is unseen, omnipresent energy, manifesting itself in various forms of measurable motion. Sound energy, produces sound waves which we experience when we hear sound, and light energy produces light waves, which are experienced in the seeing of light."

The robot stood silently, absorbing the data with computer-blowing speed and intelligence.

"Our universe is so very complex and mysterious, and many great men of science in the past realized that only God could be responsible for its existence. Isaac Newton was one - he came up with the laws of motion and the laws of gravity. He was a monotheist, a deist to be exact. He firmly believed that creation declared the existence of God. He also believed that the universe was like a machine, a clock-work universe, that ticked on a predetermined course."

"What is a monotheist, and deist?"

"Monotheism declares that there is one God. A deist believes that God created the universe and everything in it, establishing natural and moral laws. However, a deist believes that God doesn't intervene in human existence through miracles or supernatural revelation.."

There was a moment of silence.

"So God is the creator of things?"

"Yes, correct. He created a universe that is free. Man has a will, free will, that in itself is an amazing thing. And you too have free will. You can move, think and act freely. You're a very special robot, the first of your type."

The robot turned and gazed around the lab, as if testing itself.

"So why did you build me?" It raised out its hand awaiting an explanation.

Reny stood up, and placed his hand on the robot's shoulder. Its photocell eyes grew wide...

"Tell me, what's the point of my existence, my computerized world? To live, if you can even call it that, for one hundred years is pointless. I'm a computer, a machine...Nothing awaits me after I terminate."

"You were built as a result of my desire to achieve and accomplish amazing feats. You are the greatest example of what science can do for the world. You represent physics, engineering and mathematics at the highest level. You are a virtual being, with great intelligence. Your journey here might seem meaningless, but the fact that I have built a machine that can think and act accordingly, freely, surely proves that God exists. From where could man's intelligence stem from? It could only come from the divine. Also, building a machine of your calibre required a mind, intellect, calculations, thought process, so surely the atheistic world today will have to humbly accept that we humans too have a maker. Your presence alone could make people think differently. You could be the catalyst in transforming many lives. Your journey here could be far more significant and important than you think..."

Kristina

Finally it happened in the year 3000. The first human was born on Mars. The Red-Planet had finally captured its first.

Inside the gravity simulated room lay a beautiful blue-eyed baby girl. The grav-simulator worked perfectly, creating an identical gravitational field to that of earth. Of course this was fundamental for the baby's biological development and general well-being. Electrodes were attached to the baby's fragile body and head. The conduits were connected to a small sleek machine giving various readings. All encephalic data registered was perfect. Needles of the mass detectors quivered. The readings indicated excellent health.

Around her stood two female robot nurses, slender and metallic.

"Isn't she beautiful...?"

"Yes she is," it replied with electric zest.

"What a shame that her mother and father have had to return to earth..."

"I know. But remember, this was a project organised by the terra government. The parents were well paid. This project was organised purely to see how a human being would develop around robots on another planet and how she would adapt to the Martian world. Until now, only we robots have inhabited Mars. That's why we were built. Remember we robots terraformed the planet. Humans risk being here. The absence of a magnetosphere here on Mars poses serious dangers to humans. All that cosmic radiation can cause them serious harm, serious health problems and of course a weak gravitational field doesn't help any. But as long as she remains in this dome she'll be ok. Everything has been properly controlled, regulated and fixed in here. It's completely safe for her..."

Twenty years passed in a flash - at least for the golden girl Kristina. With caution she stepped out of the surface-vehicle and headed towards the church. Its old elaborate architectural design gave it sudden importance. Out in the far off distance, city lights glowed on the skyline like a frozen line of white. As she entered the church, she collapsed into a seat. Even in the dim light, she could just about make out its dimensions. Oil lamps lit up sections at intervals; such a startling contrast from the technocratic, futuristic world that lay beyond its confines. Suddenly, a pastor walked over, his features hidden in the darkness. As he approached, his elderly face became visible. He was dressed in the black classic clergyman's uniform. He had a head of fine black hair that was slowly being invaded by grey.

"Can I help you?" he said with articulate friendliness.

"Yes." Her long dark hair covered her face. Her beautiful blues eyes sparkled with tears.

"What's your name?"

"Kristina."

"How can I help you?"

There was a moment of weighted thought. Kristina looked hard into his eyes.

"I need you to answer this question..." Her beautiful chiselled face was alight with sadness... "Am I human?"

The pastor's face filled with sympathy. He stared at her as if she'd lost her mind. Kristina instantly perceived that from the look in his eyes.

"Pastor, please let me explain something to you...I was the first human to be born and brought up on Mars."

The pastor sat beside her and held her slender hand.

"I was part of a government project. I never knew my parents. I spent my first 19 and a half years living inside a huge dome. I was looked after by robots; cared for by machines. Inside the dome it was a terra like environment. Oxygen pumped. The gravity was simulated to that of Earth for proper human development. The dome was built to repel hazardous subatomic energetic particles, cosmic radiation. I was cared for in every way; had all the proper education and teaching. The robots of course taught me. However, some of my vast knowledge was implanted in me via special injections. So my knowledge was both acquired through learning and via these artificially induced injections. This gave me great scientific and mathematical understanding."

"I see," the pastor uttered softly.

"I was then transferred to Earth on a permanent basis. I have been here six months, working with the government on different space projects. Technically and legally speaking I'm human, but am I really? So now, the question I pose to you is...what am I?"

"Kristina, space and time are the framework within which the mind is constrained to construct its experience of reality, as the great philosopher Immanuel Kant once said..." He paused. "Humans need to experience the reality of the universe, the world; to see, feel, and think, and ultimately to have relationship with God. It's not dependant on where you are born, but on what you are, a tri-une being made in the image of the tri-une God, composed of body, soul and spirit. A Mars birth doesn't remove that right, the right to be human...and to be in touch with your creator, the Lord God Almighty. To know Him, is to be immortal. He is the ultimate reality."

Kristina smiled. Her smile lit up her beautiful face.

"So there's hope?"

"Yes, of course there's hope. Blood runs through your veins, your heart beats. You are human."

"Pastor, for years I struggled with this. But I simply suppressed it. It was my way of dealing with it, but psychologically it was eating me away."

"Kristina, it's understandable. But aside from your Mars birth, you must also consider this...growing up around robots for 19 and a half years would affect any human being! You needed that human connection. It's fundamental for human development, vital for psychological and emotional development. Being around inanimate objects, programmed lifeless machines, would affect anyone...No wonder you carried this burden inside your heart, the burden of whether or not you were human!"

"Of course," she responded. "Even after six months here on Earth, I still find it hard to adjust. It's been difficult relating to humans..."

"In time you will overcome this. You are now here on a permanent basis, as you said. Kristina. It's time for you to go and mix with the world; with mankind, as you have been created to do. And then you need to think about making that ultimate decision. The decision to know your Creator...no matter how far mankind advances with science and technology, man will always need God, it's etched into the very fabric of our being. Having said that, many today will still argue that God doesn't exist, but His creation reveals his glory...I'll leave you with these final words from the book of Romans 1:20; it states...*For since the creation of the world, God's invisible qualities-his eternal power and divine nature-have been clearly seen, being understood from what has been made...."*

The pastor's eyes grew wide with profundity. It was as if his eyes spoke out words of hope and love...

Moments later, Kristina walked out of the church, sharp heels clicking against the ground. Her mind began to work. She began to reflect on her years on Mars. But beyond that flash of memory, she was suddenly filled with hope. A supernatural peace surged through her. She looked up into the darkness of night. In the atmosphere, she saw a meteor tearing through the sky like a shining spear. The luminous trail it left soon faded. She now focused on the stars. God's glory was surely displayed in the wonders of space, she thought. Indeed I am human. I now have the chance to know my creator after all...

Strange Visions

The ship moved at the velocity of light. In front of the bank of controls and with articulate hands he lowered the speed of the ship. Across a screen a red light flashed – an audio voice spoke. "EVENT HORIZON – DANGER – ENTERING BLACK HOLE..." Gravity indicators quivered, indicating strong gravitational pull. In a flash of light, Prohaska suddenly found himself lying in a dimly lit room across a hygiene bed. He was totally nude and virtually unable to move, as if paralyzed by a strong narcotic. Two electrodes were attached to his head. His brain pulsed. From the electrodes, two long black conduits stretched off connecting to a large computer. Across the computer screen was a series of brain wave patterns.

"Please relax," said a cold metallic voice.

He looked up. Above him stood a robot.

"What is this? What happened? How did I get here?"

The robot moved over; a slender masterpiece of machinery, electrodes and wiring meticulously put together.

"Human – you are the only remaining one alive; the last of your kind."

"How... why?"

The robot waited a few moments before it replied.

"You have been frozen for exactly 100 years–studies in cryogenics made it possible. The world and cosmos are totally run by computers, highly advanced robots. After the war with humans, mankind was totally wiped out. You were spared. Your memory erased. Our aim was to understand the difference between the biological and mechanical. You are nothing other than a piece of flesh that will be used to undergo a vast array of experiments."

Prohaska lay there in sweat and fear. His eyes were wide open, but his gaze was fixed far beyond the ceiling wall. He battled to remember a past, who and what he was... but to no avail. The only vivid memory was his journey through space at the velocity of light, then...

"But I was on a ship entering..."

"A black hole?" The robot rasped with iron determination."A mathematically defined region of space-time?"

The robot's mind was operating on two levels simultaneously.

"Indeed... the gravitational pull is so strong that no particle or electromagnetic radiation can escape from it. But what you experienced and the only memory that you retain is actually virtual…"

"What do you mean?"

"I have been manipulating your mind, creating an artificial world…what you thought you experienced was nothing more than the manipulation of your brain chemistry. This was achieved via sending electrical signals that tamper with certain regions of the brain like the limbic system, brain stem, posterior cortex and frontal cortex. The truth is that you have been here the whole time. This proves that the human mind does indeed create reality. In fact this will open up new horizons in metaphysics…"

The robot with nimble manipulations dialled a series of numbers across the computer. At once Prohaska was propelled, travelling through the universe, his body moving like a projectile. He went to touch his face, but his hand passed through. Gripped in awe and wonder, he looked ahead into the darkness of space. He could see comets and asteroids. Seconds on, he had a birds-eye view of the Milky Way, Andromeda soon followed. Suddenly framed against the blackness of space, the universe itself, he could see images of different periods of time – Ancient Greece – Ancient Babylon, the Mongol Empire – Genghis Khan. Other images appeared… The French and American Revolutions, World Wars 1 and 2; all the pain and horror that came with it, death and destruction everywhere. Vivid pictures of Communist Russia then came into view - Lenin, Trotsky, Stalin and other members of the Bolsheviks. Then, the final devastating war between flesh and machine. Amidst the smoke and destruction the robots emerged as the new masters over planet earth. With a flash of intense light Prohaska was back on the hygiene bed, sweating profusely. The robot walked over and halted peering down at him as if looking at an inferior creature...

"Tell me Human –What is reality? What is consciousness? How can they be truly defined? Is the neural cortex the region of the brain that makes you human? Is it the region of the brain that makes Man, Man? Again what you experienced was virtual, an artificial construct. Moving through the universe seemed totally real to you. Watching relived images of the past, past worlds and civilisations, wars, dictators - the corridors of time. But it was all manufactured. The human brain is indeed a most complex organ, made up of subatomic particles, strings of light – indeed everything, all matter is made up of these oscillating strings including us robots. The human mind is no different from a hard-drive, a computer with the capacity to be fed information, and in turn create different realities, different worlds and dimensions. However, it is truly incredible how the human mind works – how it operates and functions. It is something that perhaps remains the ultimate mystery in the universe, far more complex than stellar evolution… far more complex than quantum mechanics and the universe itself. It will take our kind years to figure out all the mysteries of the human mind. Perhaps we never will…"

Temporal Transference

"Temporal Transference is the correct term," muttered Allen Buchannan boldly. "Time travel is passé. To journey back to the beginning of time and hopefully discover how our amazing planet came into existence is going to be the greatest achievement known to man."

"But with Infinite Knowledge comes infinite responsibility," Pierre responded pushing back his thick black hair.

"Indeed..."

"But Allen, are you certain it will work?"

"Of course it will. I've proven it mathematically... scientifically. Just like two masses will attract one another according to a fixed mathematical rule."

"I hope you are right…"

Silently, Allen walked around the small aluminium block (time-machine)… his grey eyes alight with pride.

"Pierre, it's incredible to think that this machine is going to move through the corridors of the past. It will create a path through the fourth dimension, a tunnel through time. It proves that consciousness can shift back and forth across time…"

"Yes, but how far back will you go? You say the beginning of time. When was that? No man could have a definitive answer. I mean....you can't be certain of when planet earth was formed."

"Indeed...when was the beginning?! That I can't answer. However I'm going to journey back to what I call Pre-man. I'll move back in time 5 million years...5 million years into the past. Who knows what I'll find..."

The next day, Allen was all set. He sat in the time machine, regulating it accordingly.

In a flash of light, as if propelled into a vortex of darkness, he moved back in time, through the fourth dimension. He held his breath, and within seconds it was over. All at once, bright sunlight filtered into the time machine. The sudden transition from darkness to bright burning sunlight stung his eyes. He battled with the glaze. Slowly the landscape around him came into focus. Awe struck, he looked around at the desolate landscape. He checked the time indicator: indeed he had made the journey back 5 million years.

He opened the side door, inched out, and stood. The sky was a pure crystal blue; a sharp contrast to the polluted skies of the future. Ahead, in the far off distance, he saw a range of mountains. The rocky landscape stretched for hundreds of miles; a vast expanse of nothing but rock and dust. He began to walk forward tentatively, almost measuring each stride, like a man who had come from another world uncertain of his surroundings. A gentle wind blew; the sound of the wind his only friend. He searched for signs of life, on the ground and in the atmosphere. Nothing moved; no signs of life anywhere. He pressed on, thoughts beginning to circle his mind...How did life begin? Who was responsible for the formation and engineering of planet earth? There's nothing here that casts any light on the whole notion of what was responsible for the dawn of man, the dawn of time. Fuelled by curiosity, he moved. Ahead in the distance he saw a huge rock. From beyond the rock, a man suddenly emerged. Paralyzed by the scene, Allen froze. His eyes widened. He was battling two opposing emotions... fear and burning curiosity. He remained still as the unknown man approached. This could be the moment that defines my journey, he thought. Within minutes the unknown man stood metres away. He was dressed in a blue robe, bare foot. His face was angelic in appearance; his skin smooth young, and clean. His brown eyes shone with a supernatural intelligence that went far beyond carnal comprehension.

Thoughts surged through Allen's mind in the moments of silence. Who is this man? Can I communicate with him...? His appearance seems out of place with this environment, this time; it's as if he doesn't belong. Within seconds...the man spoke...

"Allen who I am is not important but what I have to share with you is...."

Allen's face was flooded in amazement... How did he know my name? How did he know what I was thinking? How come he can speak to me in my language? Instantly, he knew that this man or being was no ordinary pre-historic human. He stood completely absorbed in his presence.

"Allen, what I have to say to you is of the utmost importance; fundamental to each and every human being."

He paused, staring warmly into Allen's eyes.

"Allen, Planet Earth, the universe and all life as we know originated from the one God, who is infinite in both time and space. God is a spirit, an omnipresent spirit, yet at the same time he dwells outside of space and time. He is not bound by time...hence he exists independent of the universe. He is the genesis of all life...You, and all mankind are created in His image...Was it necessary for you to journey back to try to discover who created planet earth? Your own existence, your own reality should be enough. You are a miracle, a bundle of atoms... a biological masterpiece."

Regaining his composure Allen responded, his eyes bright in the sunlight...

"Tell me, how long did it take Him to create the universe...this planet? How long did it take for Him to create man? Did He use evolution...? Did He do it over a period of billions of years? Was man slowly sculptured?

"How God chose to design the universe, and the time period it took is not important. In the book of Genesis, it makes it clear that God did it. What really should matter to Man is why...Human beings have always been concerned with how! Yes, to a certain extent asking how correlates with why...however it's clear that a divine being had to be responsible for it....that should be enough. The real question is why... Why man?"

Allen bravely responded.... "I always knew that something had to be responsible for creation. Nothing could not have created everything...Even nothing has to be something. There is no such thing as nothing...at least from a philosophical argument."

"Correct...that something is God. That is itself an admission of God's existence. Something had to be there in the beginning in order for the world to exist!"

"So why did He create human beings?"

"Relationship... God wanted relationship with Man. But simultaneously he wanted man to make a choice..."

"Free will...?"

"Yes...The essence of sin is to remove God from your life and become our own god. This is the true definition of sin...evil. Evil exists within the hearts of man. As men remove God from their life, from their existence, they fall into a dark lost world where life becomes meaningless. Slowly a Godless man withers and dies, but to them that follow God, they are filled and enriched with purpose and meaning. And beyond death awaits eternity with the eternal Creator..."

Allen stood, overwhelmed by the encounter, his eyes fixed on the unknown man.

"Allen, you must go back and tell of your experience. But change begins in you.

God is eternal, and to know Him is to be eternal..."

Suddenly the sky went black. Seconds later light appeared, the sun beaming down. The unknown man had gone. Allen turned left and right but there was no sign of him. He stood fixed on the spot, shocked, yet a strange peace encompassed him. Rapidly he rushed towards the time machine, his breath heavy, his face sweat filled. He opened the door, jumped in and sat. With nimble hands he manipulated controls, and set the time accordingly. It was time to go back and share what had happened. His eyes were filled with satisfaction. His objective had been accomplished. Before he pressed the decisive time-button, he smiled to himself... Pierre was right, he thought, with Infinite Knowledge comes infinite responsibility.

Mars

He was strapped in; strapped in hard, against the acceleration of take-off. He could move his arms freely, but his legs only to a limited extent. At once, the ship accelerated, hydraulic seats absorbing up the sudden burst of speed. Within no time the ship began its journey through the blackness of space that separated Mars from earth. Greg Robinson stretched out his arms, touching the hemisphere of information devices that engulfed him. He manipulated controls and fiddled with dials that controlled the viewscope. It was all bathed in light; a mild glow of lights which were powered by electricity from the solar batteries. The batteries themselves had been exposed to burning sunlight. It never failed. The spin of the ship produced a centrifugal force that pressed him down in his seat. He felt his weight...it felt like he was on earth...exposed to its gravitational force. Fixed across the external body of the ship, and positioned neatly, were photoelectric cells. They whirled constantly, scanning space. He leaned back, calm and composed. He studied the viewscope. It appeared brighter against the deepening contrast of darkness...space. A reading appeared: Mars – Earth currently at their closest points: Total Distance 56 million Kilometres. Journey time: approximately six months. He slipped into a shallow sleep, thoughts of earth and its beauty swimming in his mind. He would soon be there. A sudden thought of not making it struck him. But he briskly pushed it aside; based purely on the law of probability and statistics.

Seven months elapsed…..

"It was an experience like no other," Greg exclaimed, his eyes full of expression. "Trudging on the Martian ground was quite something…the months of preparation and psychotherapy certainly helped…"

He paused for a few seconds scratching his square jaw.

"After a month out there, you slowly adjust to the weaker gravitational field of the planet. Coming back to Earth and adapting to normality is kind of strange after spending two years on the Red Planet…"

"I've noticed it," laughed Bill, "I've noticed it in your movements, in that somewhat tentative walk of yours….So, tell me, can we terraform Mars?"

"Definitely, however one negative thing is that Mars lost its magnetosphere approximately 4 billion years ago."

"Reason…?"

"I'd say due to numerous asteroid strikes…as a result, the solar wind interacts directly with the Martian ionosphere.

Basically, there's no protection from cosmic radiation...However, we can terraform the planet; no question."

Greg sat on his large office chair tilting back...his hands pressed together in deep contemplation.

"There are several proposed concepts....and it is important that we commence this project soon....remember Bill, the Future population of this planet will grow to enormous numbers, hence we need to colonize other planets beginning with Mars. It is the most Earth-like of all the other planets in the Solar System."

"Yes indeed," Bill muttered. "Given the similarities and proximity, Mars would be the best target."

"Well Bill, I'll start with the negatives....The low gravity could cause many health problems; the surface-gravity is 38% of that on Earth. Another point is that the lower gravity of Mars requires 2.6 times Earth's column air-mass to obtain100 kPa pressure at the surface. Then there's the problem of space weather... as mentioned Mars lacks a magnetosphere, hence the planet is bombarded with cosmic radiation...this is a serious health risk for humans...there are many hazardous consequences...cancers, etc. Also, the lack of a magnetosphere could also pose problems in retaining an atmosphere...in time, solar winds could tear away the atmosphere."

He stood up and walked towards the window, gazing towards the distant flickers of starlight….

"Now for the positives…The Martian world, I mean its atmosphere and soil contain many of the main elements crucial to life; for example: carbon, sulphur, nitrogen, hydrogen, oxygen. Also, vast amounts of water ice exist below the Martian surface. Electrolysis is a great way to separate water on Mars. As a DC current passes through the water (solution) it separates the oxygen atoms and the hydrogen atoms. Obviously, sufficient liquid water and electricity has to be available…The problem is, that once Mars has an atmosphere, retaining that atmosphere may be a problem. The planet's gravitational field is not strong enough to retain an atmosphere. In time, it could be lost to outer space. Hence, the key in retaining the atmosphere is… we must keep the planet warm. In any case: Terraforming entails the following changes: firstly building up the atmosphere, by heating up the planet (greenhouse effect) and as explained keeping it warm, and keeping the atmosphere from being lost to outer space.

"I hear that importing ammonia could help?"

"Yes Bill, indeed. Importing ammonia could help terraform the planet, no question. Ammonia is a powerful greenhouse gas. Also, importing hydrocarbons…methane is another greenhouse gas. Use of orbital mirrors is also very effective. It would maximize sunlight absorption, as a result it would heat the planet, melting the ice-caps and slowly releasing CO_2. Obviously, Mars's surface temperature would increase...reducing the albedo of the Martian surface would make more efficient use of incoming sunlight. The ground would then absorb more sunlight, as a result it would warm the atmosphere..."

"It all sounds wonderful....but can it really be achieved?"

"As I said Bill, yes, it can. Lots of money will have to be injected into this amazing project, which will take years..."

"You know Grieg, one important, in fact, vital question is... how will man adapt to the Martian world? Of course as you mentioned, there are many possible dangers, health hazards, like cosmic radiation and adjusting to the weaker gravitational field. But what I want to know is...over time, mankind will change, evolve; biological, psychological and neurological changes are certain to take place. Hence, I guess that the biggest metaphysical question that will need to be answered is: will the humans that are born on Mars be considered human? Will mankind lose its identity? Remember we are our environment. Our environment shapes us. Terraformed or not, Mars remains an alien world. What will become of man? Again I ask you...will humans that are born of Mars be considered human? Perhaps at first, yes, but over time who knows...?"

The Tide of Time

"Time," said Martin Claus, leaning across his desk toward the small group of seated students, their eyes ablaze with penetrating interest. "Travelling in time, means travelling in the fourth dimension...Portals to the past and future are possible through the laws of nature. Wormholes occur in space-time, and they constantly form within the quantum world."

He straightened himself, brushed back his thick grey hair and sat down on his chair.

"Professor, could a giant wormhole be constructed in space... I mean, do you really think it is possible to enter a wormhole and travel back in time?

"I'm not certain Larry..." he replied, crossing his legs with an elaborated casualness.

"Tell me, didn't Einstein say... that every bit of time exists right here, right now?"

"Yes Larry, the implications are that we exist at different moments in this space-time continuum, and that the past, and the future, exist as much as the present."

"What about unlocking that gateway, say into the future?"

"Well," he responded somewhat enigmatically, drumming his fingers on the desk, "time, if you like, flows like a river. It flows at different speeds in different places...hence, time is relative. This is the key to travelling into the future. For example, time appears to run faster in space and slower down on earth. This makes time travel into the future possible. If you place a clock in a gravitational field, as the clock gets closer to the gravitational field, the clock will slow down. Up in space it speeds up....Basically gravity has an effect on time."

His dark wise eyes widened across his old intellectual face, as he paused momentarily.

"A black hole can also be looked at as a natural time – machine. A black hole slows time down; it basically has an effect on time. As you get closer to a black hole, you will start to experience a greater gravitational pull. If a space ship were to carefully orbit a black hole making all the right calculations, i.e. trajectory and velocity, for a period of time, the crew on board would experience time slowed down. The implications are that they would then return to a future earth, where a greater amount of time would have elapsed... Basically, the crew would have made a journey in both space and time. Then of course the most plausible way of journeying into the future would be to travel at the speed of light. One year on board a ship moving through space at that velocity, would mean returning to a world where ten years would have elapsed..."

"Interesting," said Larry.

"Then finally, another Time machine if you like, is the Hadron Collider, the particle accelerator. They take protons and accelerate them to almost the velocity of light... then smash them together. As a result subatomic particles are formed out of the explosion. They live for a billionth of a second. But in the particle accelerator, a billionth of a second is stretched out relative to our time...Basically the particle accelerator turns atoms into Time Travellers."

"So Professor, you believe it is possible to journey into the future from a scientific perspective, not just theory?"

"Yes Larry, absolutely... Another interesting point I'd like to make is, most scientists tend to believe that the entire universe; the entire four dimensional space-time that we all exist in, is equally real. That is, we exist at different moments in this space-time continuum. Most physicists tend to be eternalists."

Through the window, a beam of sunlight shone across his face, as the sun escaped the clouds.

"Your vast array of knowledge is remarkable Professor......."

"That's kind Larry," he responded in an avuncular manner. "But the truth is, the more you learn, the more you realise that you ultimately know nothing. That is, the immense knowledge that you think you have attained, is non-existent relative to the mysteries of science and the universe that stretch far beyond man. There is so much more to discover. Things that our minds will never get to fully understand, at least in this dimension...."

"This dimension...? Sorry what do you mean Professor?"

"Beyond this three dimensional space, exists an eternal dimension..."

"Really, you believe that?" he replied with distant amusement."

"Yes...remember energy cannot be destroyed. You are energy. That proves that one, we are immortal, and two, there has to be another dimension beyond this three dimensional space. There is a spark, a fire within us that lives on beyond our physical selves."

"So you believe in the soul, a Spirit?"

"Yes...some describe the soul as a nexus of electromagnetic forces. Whatever the case, and however you want to define it, I believe that after death you have the capacity for thought, memories, and personality. If you like, the essence of your brain remains permanent. Think about this: what really makes you, you? All matter is energy made up of atoms. Consciousness arises as a result of billions of neurons at work, giving rise to thought. The brain is a self aware piece of soft tissue that is so complex, perhaps the most complex piece of matter within the cosmos. It is a computer of nerve cells, neurons, that when they interact with each other, become a self aware symbiotic network. However, the definition of the soul goes far deeper than that. There is no doubt in my mind that the soul is built from something more fundamental than neurons. It is not a fading illusion as many think; it does outlive the physical network, and in fact lives on eternally."

The Professor paused, for a few seconds...

"Many philosophers today, believe that consciousness creates the universe, that the body and brain are a spatial temporal construct. For example, when we sleep, our mind creates space and time... without space and time nothing really exists. The questions that metaphysics raises are so vital and so very important. Again, many philosophers today argue that the soul is constructed from the fabric of the universe, and that consciousness is an integral part of the universe. Many say that consciousness is a quantum process and that the soul is a quantum computer hardwired into the universe. Regardless of all this, I believe that consciousness does require a complex convoluted system and mechanism to support it. I believe that the cerebral cortex is wired up appropriately to create consciousness...and that ultimately, to truly define man, the soul, and consciousness you have to enter into the realms of theology."

"Professor, I've always wondered about the nature of reality. I mean...do we really see the universe as it is? Or is it all in our minds? Do our senses betray us? Is reality nothing other than a computer simulator? Perhaps the brain is wired in such a way that it processes information that it wants us to see? Is our existence and reality just an illusion? Are we blinded to the true nature of reality?"

"Larry, our perceptions and our senses are very limited. Science tells us that there are hidden realities, like the quantum world we have being discussing. There are subatomic levels of reality. The subatomic world does not obey the laws of physics. It has its own laws. It is a reality of its own. However, the best way to deal with the whole notion of reality is this... Our universe is only a small part of a much larger reality. Going back to what I said before, energy cannot be destroyed, hence, we are eternal in nature; this implies that there has to be an eternal dimension after death, a whole new world...a new universe if you like."

"So you believe in a God then?"

"Yes, indeed. Man was made in His image, the infinite and eternal One. What God knows is infinite. Hence, what there is to know must also be infinite."

The professor now stood up from the chair with purpose, yet with considerable composure. His eyes appeared to smile, even though his lips didn't.

"What is God professor, and how did He come into existence?"

"God, by definition, means the eternal one. So your question in essence is totally illogical....an oxymoron. You see, atheism makes no sense. How could the universe and all life have come into existence from nothing? We live in a universe of cause and effect; it's the fundamental rule of science. Something had to cause the universe to come into existence. For example, can 0x0=everything? An atheist says yes. But that simple mathematical equation that I just gave is utter nonsense, and yet it runs parallel with atheistic thinking. What seems logical to an atheist, can lose out in the basic mathematical equation."

There were a few moments of silence.

"The universe is so finely designed, it's simply astonishing. Take celestial mechanics. How planets move and operate. Take our moon, centred in unstable equilibrium. If it were to slow down it would move away from Earth. Speed up, and it would come closer towards our planet. Everything is so finely balanced."

The Professor sat down on his chair, his shrewd eyes, once again weighing his quality and deep intellect. He licked his thin lips...

"I'll end with this...God dwells outside of space and time. Hence, he is eternal in nature. Entropy has no effect on Him. He is the catalyst behind entropy. We all die, everything on earth and within the cosmos. There is cosmic death, stars, etc...The tide of time eats away at everything. Nothing can stand against it. But the Tide of Time has no effect on the eternal everlasting God that exists independent of the universe for all time......"

Infinity begins tomorrow

It was night on Mars. The Martian world was silent. The 24 hour, 40 minute day cycle was almost over. Inside his large mansion lay Walter Dugan; the man that had been responsible for terraforming the planet along with a team of elite scientists and engineers. He controlled much of what happened on the planet in terms of the scientific aspects, such as maintaining the atmosphere. The weak gravitational field of the planet meant that the atmosphere was in danger of being lost to outer space. It had to be constantly replenished and kept warm. In honour of what he had done, the main city centre bore his name: Dugan City.

Lying quietly on his bed, he called out to the servant.

"Luke....I haven't got long."

"It's here Sir, just arrived."

"It...! What do you mean?"

A tall robot walked into the dimly lit room. In the terra-simulated gravity field of the mansion its steps thundered as it moved closer to the bed.

"Professor Dugan, I'm Hosea, an x-robot of the highest kind. I hear that you haven't got long."

Walter looked up at the robot, his aged eyes dimly alert.

"Yes, days if that.... I knew that the only group that could possibly help me was the newly formed theological society here on Mars. The only thing that I didn't expect was a robot."

"Why, Professor Dugan...?"

"Because you're a machine..... What could you tell me about death?"

"Yes indeed Professor Dugan, I'm a machine, built from miniaturised gearboxes and motors, thanks to the advances in materials such as magnesium alloys and neodymium magnets. I'm a complex network of carbon-fibre composites, advanced metal alloys and special plastics. Carbon nanotubes give me unlimited strength... Brushless servomotors regulate my motion accuracy. Everything is indeed mechanical...."

"So you can think, can you?"

"Professor Dugan, this great philosophical question of whether or not a computer can think was raised centuries ago on planet Earth. At its core, the science of Artificial Intelligence is the quest to understand the very mechanisms of intelligence. Intelligence in a human being or a machine can be defined as the ability to solve problems and achieve certain tasks."

The robot paused, staring at Walter with deep perception...

"For many years now, man has studied cognitive psychology - how humans think, and attempted to write mathematical formulas - algorithms, that mimic the logical mechanisms of human intelligence. These algorithms – bits of programming logic, instruct us machines how to act and be and it works amazingly well. It allows us to identify related concepts and make the kind of intuitive connections we call experience. Probability is a massive component of higher-level machine reasoning, using unprecedented processing power to give the most likely answer from a virtually limitless range of knowledge. Robots like me have proven to be highly intelligent and logical, solving the most complex of equations."

"Look I needed a human."

"Please professor, allow me to finish..."

"Have you ever played a game of chess against a machine – a robot? You will never win, not even you. A robot like me for example, can calculate a nearly infinite number of moves and countermoves. The way we process information is quite unbelievable. Alternatively, please consider this: look at the special navigation systems that you use when travelling through space. Speak your destination, the on-board computer will interpret your voice, locate your exact spatial location, and then give you detailed directions. It can even take you where you want via the autonomic circuit."

The robot paused moving closer to the bed....

"When I walk, I use infrared and ultrasonic sensors to gauge distances from floors, walls and moving objects, and constantly adjust my balance and motion with 34 high – precision servo motors. I'm equipped with an internal gyroscope and speed sensor that helps me achieve balance at all times, and in all situations. Special sensors regulate the amount of force that I apply depending on the task. Through radio sensors I can read data on magnetic ID cards. Sensors in my feet and hands help me to feel the six axes of force."

"But you are programmed...."

"Man is programmed too, biologically. The human brain is a profoundly complex machine. Professor, what is thought? It is such a vague and subjective term. Perhaps what should be asked is: can a machine imitate the way humans interact? The answer is yes! What is common sense? It's a combination of stored knowledge, logical reasoning, probability and language interpretation. A robot has the capacity to execute all those with lightning speed. Machines have been programmed to reason. Computers are brilliant statisticians, and with the right algorithms, we can quickly make billions of calculations to decide which answer or action is most likely to produce the desired result. We are highly logical, programmed to recognise that if 1 and 2 are true, then the only logical conclusion is 3. We make decisions based on evidence and probability. This is due to mathematical models which in turn create logical processes. Computer programming languages are grounded in logic. This is the only way we robots can learn....Now, let's get back to you."

Walter looked up at the machine, with a look of resignation. His face was yellow and gaunt. His lined forehead dripped with sweat.

"The reason I called, is because I'm dying. I'm an atheist... I struggle with the whole concept of God, and an afterlife....I want to believe but I can't. I want to call out to Him, if He exists...but I can't. How can you help me to see, given that my life is coming to an end?"

"God loves you Professor. You need to call out to Him. He wants you to love Him freely. It's a choice. Remember the past is the key to the present; that is, the story of Adam and Eve, whether or not taken literally, is a day to day reflection of Man. That is, each day Man is challenged morally. Each day man has to make decisions pertaining to ethics. Man was intrinsically designed to have free will and decide between right and wrong. Now, you need to reach out to Him. Ask Him for forgiveness, because no matter how good man thinks he is, man falls way short of Godly standards. This is why Man needed a saviour. Now is the time to reach out to Him, and ask Him into your life!"

The Robot raised its hand.....

"Look at all the false human philosophies. They have all failed. Man attempted to redefine God. For example, Panentheism: god is in all. Pantheism: all is god. This is an absolute distortion of what God is. He is creator... period! As for the other false philosophies: Animism: sprits are god. Atheism: no God. Agnosticism: don't know. Polytheism: many gods. Dualism: two gods, good and bad. Deism: God exists, but He can't control His creation. Monotheism: one God. Existentialism: religious experience is god. Humanism: man is god. Rationalism: reason is god, that is, the only things that are true are things that can be proven. Materialism: only matter is real. Mysticism: only spirit is real. Monism: matter and spirit are one and the same in essence. Now the only one that comes close to the truth is Theism in the general term: That is, God exists and can control His creation. This is one step towards biblical philosophy."

"But I can't accept the creation account in Genesis..."

"Professor that was written in a way to reach out to all....It was written with simplicity. The six days of creation don't have to be taken literally. They could be considered to be six geological days. Remember, God is outside time.

However time is real to God, but it is also relative to God. The point is this: God made the universe, how long it took doesn't matter. The one message is that God made everything! In Genesis, God takes three days to form the world, and three to inhabit it. First three days, God creates the environment, the other three days... He creates life to inhabit that environment. God brings order out of chaos. He does it mathematically. First, He separates light from darkness, sky from Ocean, and land from sea. Then, He creates Sun and Moon, and stars, then birds and fish...and then finally, animals and human beings. "

"But what about science...?"

"Professor, Science and God don't have to be segregated, they need to be integrated. Yes, science studies the natural world, physical truth; it can't study the supernatural realm, spiritual truth. However Science and God can live together. After all God is the Greatest Scientist of all. He created the laws of the universe. Furthermore, Science agrees exactly with the order of Genesis.... The original earth was covered with a thick mist. When the plants came and started changing carbon dioxide into oxygen, it cleared the mist. And for the first time, the Sun and Moon and stars appeared in the heavens. The bible account fits in perfectly with Science..."

A few seconds of silence passed...

"Professor please note: science is transitional. It's constantly changing. The atom was considered the smallest thing in the universe. Now, we know about sub-atomic particles...the atom, is a whole universe in itself. Geology changes too. There are many ways to establish the age of the earth: Magnetic field decay, Carbon 14, etc. Their readings all vary. My point is that, science has transformed our world but it's not always right. It changes constantly. Look at man; the complexity of man. God is behind science. Take DNA! DNA, was the most complex form of life, and the earliest form. DNA is a language; it is not a chance combination, but a language. It passes information from one generation to another. Therefore, DNA must have a person behind it...a mechanism. Look at the cell structure... the cell membrane: it's the covering of what enters and leaves the cell. Chromosomes.... contain the cell's DNA. Mitochondria...supplies energy for the cell. Look at the design of life in general: On planet Earth microscopic bacteria preceded man by thousands of years in making a rotary engine. One bacterium has hair-like extensions twisted together to form a stiff spiral. It spins this corkscrew around like the propeller of a ship and drives itself forward. It can even reverse its engine. How? The sonar of a bat surpasses man. Look at jet propulsion in animals. Take the octopus and squid: They suck water into a special chamber and then, with powerful muscles, expel it. This propels them forward. Approximately 500 varieties of electric fish have batteries. Take the giant electric ray of the

North Atlantic based on planet Earth. It puts out 50-ampere pulses of 60 volts. The African cat-fish can produce 350 volts. A rattle snake has pits on the sides of its head with which it can sense a change of 1/600 degree Fahrenheit. A boa constrictor responds in 35 milliseconds to a heat change of a fraction of a degree. Microscopic radiolarians have oil droplets in their protoplasm by which they regulate their weight and thereby move up or down in the ocean. Fish diffuse gas into or out of their swim bladders, altering buoyancy. All chance...? No, God is behind all life....Now, why the problem of evil? Human philosophy tries to explain it. Evil exists due to dualism. Good and bad God. Evil isn't something physical or moral. It is the material source of the universe that is evil. In personal terms, the body is the source of temptation. The other human notion is that evil doesn't exist. There are only evil people. Evil is not a thing that exists on its own. But the bible tells us that evil originated with Satan. The best definition of evil is this: Men wanting to be their own god, hence, removing God from their lives. Finally, nothing can't create everything: that is something had to be there in the beginning for there to be everything that we see today. Only an eternal God could have been responsible. All the great philosophers of ancient Greece believed that something was always there in the beginning. That is, the universe always existed in some form, energy etc....They couldn't accept that from nothing came everything. Something had to be there in the beginning. In a sense they are correct. However that something could only be God. But He created everything out of nothing. Ask yourself this: from where did energy come? The amount of energy in this universe is constant. It changes form but it is the same. So from where did it come? God put it into the system – that is the open system, the universe."

The robot paused momentarily in mechanical reflection.....

"Professor," it said softly. "It all comes down to this: Man dies; beyond death, man stands before God. They will either enter into an eternity of hell – separation from God, or an eternity of heaven – a place where they will spend all eternity with God. The choice is yours.... the only difference between a robot and a human being is this: Man lives on beyond death eternally, and has the capacity to know God. A robot has an expiry date, beyond that we cease to exist. You are eternal. Life, your existence here, is just an illusion compared with what lies beyond."

The professor gazed towards the window at the Martian world he had created. His eyes were filled with hope and an unusual energy which seemed to consume the actual organ of sight itself. Slowly, and with care, the robot knelt beside the bed and stretched out its arm. Its hand rested on the professor's shoulder.

"It's time to choose professor. Death is just the beginning. Infinity begins tomorrow...."

PLATO 5

Dr. Edward P. Clarke sat in deep thought. As a retired physicist deep thinking was not alien to him. Sitting in his office at home he gazed towards the fireplace where a warm bright firelight burned. Through the long minutes of tranquillity, a sudden ring severed the deep silence of night. Edward stood up and walked with purpose towards the phone, cold moonlight filtering in through the window.

"Edward, it's complete. The official name - Plato 5. It's technically perfect. Works like clock-work!"

"Fantastic news," he responded, scratching his bald aged head.

"Ed, this machine will revolutionize the world, solve the most complex equations, answer man's deepest questions. It will give us great mathematical details about how antigravity is possible, revolutionizing spacecraft propulsion. This machine is an entity of its own."

"Great. So, when can I test it?"

"1pm tomorrow, at the university."

"Perfect, I'll be there."

Edward disconnected. His eyes narrowed with a duality of belief and doubt. If this computer does work, the implications for humanity are vast, he thought.

12.55pm the next day, Edward arrived at the Massachusetts Institute of Technology. He sat inside a large dark chamber, only metres from Plato 5. Behind it, row after row of electrical equipment stretched. The bland grey computer itself was nothing special in terms of its design and structure. Visually it appeared very basic, mundane and uninspiring. This prompted further doubt is his mind.

"Arthur, are you certain..."

Before he could finish, Arthur suavely interrupted.

"Ed old boy trust me. Years of mind breaking sweat went into this project."

He paused reflectively, his light blue eyes full of confidence.

"Why don't you start by asking it questions you know the answers to. You'll soon discover how precise and efficient it is."

Arthur threw a switch activating the computer. The room was suddenly filled with a raucous whining sound. Seconds later it stilled into silence. The large screen slowly lit up. At first a dull glow. Words then appeared: FIRST QUESTION.

Edward adjusted himself.

"Good day Plato-5."

"Good day to you," it replied with a soft male humanoid voice."

Edward licked his lips.

"Plato-5, can you please tell me how fast the speed of light is?"

"Its value is exactly 299,792,458 metres per second."

The cold hazy light beaming from the screen lit up Arthur's skeletal, bony face as he turned, staring at Edward with a glint of delight. Edward considered his next question, rubbing his aged hands.

"What's Albert Einstein's famous equation?"

"$E=mc^2$."

"What does it mean?

"E stands for energy and m stands for mass, a measurement of the quantity of matter. The c stands for the speed of light, a universal constant. The equation simply breaks down to this: energy is equal to matter multiplied by the speed of light squared."

"Ask it a few more general questions, and then you can really start," exclaimed Arthur.

"What's the value of Pi?"

"3.14159265359."

"Who was Archimedes?"

"Archimedes of Syracuse was an Ancient Greek mathematician, physicist, engineer, inventor, and astronomer."

Edward rubbed his broad jaw, satisfied and impressed.

"Is the Sun magnetically active?"

"Yes, the Sun is a magnetically active star."

"What is the sun primarily composed of?"

"It is composed primarily of the chemical elements hydrogen 74.9% and helium 23.8%."

"Perfect," Edward muttered quietly under his breath.

"Give me its diameter?"

"It has a diameter of about 865,374 miles. That equates to 1,392,684 km."

"Give me Earth's escape velocity?"

"From the surface of the Earth, escape velocity is about 25,000 miles per hour... 7 miles per second."

"Marvellous Plato-5, marvellous..."

"What did I tell you," chirped Arthur. "It's unbelievable. Continue..."

Edward contemplated silently. I need to give it a more testing question, a question that will demand thought, an opinion...its opinion, as opposed to a straight forward answer.

"Plato-5, in your opinion, who was the greatest philosopher of all time?"

There was a delay in its response. The atmosphere was building as they both awaited its well-calculated opinion.

"The German philosopher Friedrich Wilhelm Nietzsche."

Edward immediately understood the implications of its answer. Intrigue manifested itself across his face.

"Arthur, this computer is atheistic in nature...."

A few seconds of weighted silence passed...

"Plato-5, are you suggesting that nothing created everything?"

"Your question is misleading. What I'm suggesting is that there is no such thing as a creator."

"So, what was responsible for the birth of the universe, the creation of man, this three dimensional space we inhabit?"

"An explosion formed our universe. Millions of years of evolution brought man into existence. "

"You mean the big bang theory?"

"Correct. The age of the universe is approximately 13.8 billion years.

After the initial explosion and expansion, the universe cooled sufficiently. As a result subatomic particles were formed."

"Plato-5, the theory postulates that at some point in time all space was contained in a single point. After the explosion the universe has been expanding ever since. This is quite a mind-blowing event. The question I raise is if this is true, what was responsible for it? What was the trigger mechanism? Something had to be responsible for this highly complex convoluted process, surely?"

"To ask what caused the Big Bang is meaningless."

Edward looked at Arthur, somewhat perturbed by the insufficient response.

"Plato-5, I think that's a very important question to answer, in fact fundamental. If you postulate that the universe came into existence via an explosion, you should have some idea of what caused it? All events have causes!"

"To ask what caused the big bang is not a question that can be rationally, scientifically and intellectually answered."

"Plato-5, if the cosmos and all life originated with the big bang, surely the greatest metaphysical question for mankind to answer is what caused it? How can that be considered a meaningless, non-intellectual question? The key to our existence lies in the answer."

"Science has already answered all the questions. I work on a scientific basis, an intellectual and logical perspective only, not a theological one."

Edward's eyes lit up! "Theological, what makes you think and say that?"

Plato-5 didn't respond.

"If the big bang can only be explained from a theological perspective as you have just indicated and in fact indirectly stated, then you yourself have confirmed that only a creator could have logically been responsible for such an event. You have categorically confirmed it with your last statement even though you reject the whole notion as a result of your atheistic view. Your whole argument and rejection of God is based on this false doctrine."

Arthur gazed over at Edward in stunned silence. Edward continued...

"Plato-5, the more we understand science, the more we realize that there has to be a mechanism behind it in order for it to work so efficiently. Science has got be the greatest proof of God's existence. Take quantum mechanics, the study of subatomic particles...strings of light that oscillate. Indeed everything within our universe oscillates. Take Fractal Geometry, Fractals...the fingerprints of God...The Colours of Infinity. Fractal geometry has made it possible to mathematically explore nature. It helps us understand our world, our universe...at a subatomic level."

The computer suddenly ceased operating. Its hazy light promptly faded. Arthur lowered his head and with his hand rubbed his forehead in disappointment, his thick gold ring large and distinct.

"Arthur, I'm sorry but as brilliant as Plato-5 is or was, with all its scientific knowledge and insight in physics, biology, chemistry and astrophysics, when it came down to answering the most important and vital metaphysical question of all…it simply failed!

"It appears so," replied Arthur, his confidence somewhat regained, evident by the gleam in his eyes.

"Atheism, as you have seen, has no fundamental foundation. It hovers hopelessly without a base. As we've discussed countless times, the whole notion of a creator being solely responsible for creation of the cosmos and all life as we know it, is the only logical answer. We both remain theists, but the next step in our journey is to discover who this creator really is…"

Lightning Source UK Ltd.
Milton Keynes UK
UKOW02f2355251116
288598UK00001B/14/P